The Suicides
Jenna Wimshurst

Copyright © 2019 by Jenna Wimsurst

All rights reserved. No part of this publication may be reproduced, stored or transmitted in any form or by any means, electronic, mechanical, photocopying, recording, scanning, or otherwise without written permission from the publisher. It is illegal to copy this book, post it to a website, or distribute it by any other means without permission.

This novel is entirely a work of fiction. The names, characters and incidents portrayed in it are the work of the author's imagination. Any resemblance to actual persons, living or dead, events or localities is entirely coincidental.

Jenna Wimsurst asserts the moral right to be identified as the author of this work.

Jenna Wimsurst has no responsibility for the persistence or accuracy of URLs for external or third-party Internet Websites referred to in this publication and does not guarantee that any content on such Websites is, or will remain, accurate or appropriate.

Designations used by companies to distinguish their products are often claimed as trademarks. All brand names and product names used in this book and on its cover are trade names, service marks, trademarks and registered trademarks of their respective owners. The publishers and the book are not associated with any product or vendor mentioned in this book. None of the companies referenced within the book have endorsed the book.

First edition

To my darling Suz, thank you for being so amazing. I love you

1

Prologue

It was just after lunchtime on another tedious Tuesday when I finally decided that it was time to kill myself. I've got depression, you see. 'Who hasn't?' I hear you cry. Well, if you could keep the crying to a minimum while you're reading this book that would be great, thank you.

I've had depression all my life but unfortunately it had recently been made worse when I discovered my father swinging from the garage ceiling. Whether or not he had planned for me to be the one who found him is unclear, but I had been the only person he'd invited around for dinner that evening, so the odds of it being me who found him were, you could say, ridiculously high.

Inside my bathroom medicine cabinet were two Tupperware boxes full of tablets. The large box was full of feeble tablets and jumbo plasters while the smaller one contained the harder drugs. I grabbed the smaller box, went into my bedroom and shut the door...

2

Sandra

Do you know what I love more than sitting at home, getting pissed on cheap wine while watching QI? Absolutely nothing; in fact, what I've just described to you is my favourite thing to do. But for some reason I've decided not to do that and to instead spend my time standing in the fucking rain, on a bridge, trying to stop some man I don't know from killing himself.

I saw him from my car as I'd been waiting for the traffic lights to turn green. I would've just left him to jump but I suspected that he didn't know that the bridge wasn't high enough to kill him. Did he know that he was about to paralyse himself, leaving a terrible mess that would be absolute hell for everyone involved?

Was he definitely trying to kill himself though? He could just be some drunken twat hanging out on a bridge. But if he wasn't just some drunken twat, then he would soon be a paralysed twat, and for some bizarre reason I felt obligated to warn him.

'He'd better be trying to kill himself,' I said to myself as I put my hood up and got out of my car.

The wind was fierce as it smashed against my tired, pale face. It was as if the weather was deliberately mocking me as I walked onto the bridge and towards the man. Now that I could see the way that he was looking down and sobbing loudly, it was obvious that he was wanting to jump.

Thank fuck for that! I don't get embarrassed easily, but it would've been slightly awkward if I'd approached him and told him not to jump, only to find out that he was some teenager Instagramming the river below.

'Are you going to jump or what?' I shouted, as if I'd just asked him for the time. He ignored me. 'I was actually on my way home to get plastered in front of the telly, so could we hurry this up?' The man turned his head to the side slightly.

'Go away!' he shouted back, his voice cracking at the end. Oh *great*, he's emotional. Dealing with emotional people is *definitely* one of my favourite past times - like being sober, or spending time with loved ones.

I wasn't going to go away but I knew that I had to tread carefully because he might jump at any minute, and something inside me wanted to stop him from doing that. Don't get me wrong, it wasn't because I wanted him to live - please, I couldn't give two shits. But I knew that a fall from the 80-foot bridge wasn't likely to kill him. People jumped off the Golden Gate bridge and survived all the time, so there was no question that jumping off Malford bridge was probably not going to have the desired outcome.

'Your organs will impact the water a fraction of a second after your body does. It'll rip your aorta clean from your heart, killing you very quickly!' I yelled at him. 'Well, it would if you were jumping from the Beipanjiang in southern China.' I stuffed my hands in my pockets, struggling to keep still in the strong evening wind.

'I read that it's like hitting the pavement. So quick that I won't feel anything!' he shouted back.

'Wrong!' I huffed, irritated. This was already becoming tedious, especially with all the bloody shouting. 'The bridge isn't high enough for that; you'll feel every bit of the impact! Your ribs will break and puncture your lungs, your organs will hit the wall of your body and if you're *really* lucky, it will kill you! But given the shortness of the drop, you're more likely to just paralyse yourself; someone will have to feed you, wipe your dribbly willy and clean the skank out of your belly button... unless that was what you were hoping would happen?' I shouted, as I swept a wet clump of hair away from my face.

The man didn't respond. He was probably thinking about what and why I had just shouted at him. He was busy preparing himself to jump off the bridge before I came along, and he obviously hadn't even thought about what would happen if he fucked up his suicide attempt. In fact, I'd probably made him feel worse than he had when he'd first stepped onto the bridge; just one of my many special talents.

'Why can't you just sod off?' he yelled, his voice cracking at the end.

'Because I've got out of my car now and although I had planned to get wet this evening, it was supposed to be in the privacy of my own home, not with a stranger on a bridge.'

'Are you a police officer?'

'Do I look like a police officer?'

'I can't see in the dark!' he snapped.

'No, I'm not a police officer. I'm just some woman who was on her way home from the offy, looking forward to an evening of light entertainment and a drunken fiddle before bed.' A noise escaped the man. It sounded like a laugh, but I couldn't for the life of me see what was funny.

He kept his eyes glued to the water below.

'Come over to this side of the railings and let me help you!' I shouted, becoming more fed up with this stupid toing and froing.

'With what? Therapy?' he laughed. 'Therapy can't help me now!'

We both fell silent for a few minutes, giving me more than enough time to decide that even though I didn't want him to end up paralysed, I really couldn't be bothered with this anymore. I did actually want to help the bloke.

'I can help you kill yourself.'

'Oh, for God's sake, Sandra! There are three bottles of Pinot, four recorded episodes of QI and some quality alone time waiting for you at home.'

I had no idea what I was saying or where this need to help someone other than myself had come from; I guess it made a nice change from my usual cold-hearted, bitchy self. *'I should call my mother and tell her immediately,'* I thought. She'd be thrilled to know that she hadn't raised a totally soulless child.

So, how would I help him? It would be a bit stupid of me to give him an overdose, considering my past, but the list of other methods that I could think of weren't exactly helpful either. There was the noose, the gun, the slit wrists and the toxic car fumes. The gun method was out of the question because I had no idea where to get one from. After all, this was the small Surrey town of Malford, not a school town in Florida. Also, I wouldn't want to see someone hanging again and nor did I want someone dying in my lovely Volvo, unless we used his car. But there was that bizarre suicide bag that Mary had mentioned...

The man turned his head back around to get a proper look at my face. I was cold, wet and very close to the end of my tether. I slowly walked closer to him.

'Why don't you-'.

'Stay back!' he cried, shooting one hand out and stopping me in my tracks.

He began to wobble slightly. Was it panic or the wind? His foolproof plan had holes in it now, thanks to me. I felt a bit sorry for him in a way - he just wanted to die and here I was, trying to talk him down like some kind of care in the community shit.

'Alright, just calm yourself, I'm only walking to sit on the bench,' I said, moving over to the bench that was just to the left of him. *'Because I can see this is going to take a-fucking-while,'* I muttered to myself, as I plonked my arse on the seat. He turned his head to the side so that he could see my face properly.

'How do I know I can trust you?' he said at a normal volume, now that I was a lot closer to him.

'Well-'

'If *you* failed at doing it, then how are you going to make sure that *I* do it properly?' he interrupted. I waited a while before answering. I don't take kindly to being interrupted. Suicidal or not, don't fucking interrupt me.

'So, you know who I am,' I said. He nodded.

'Your face was all over the newspaper.'

'Well, I was impulsive and I didn't have the right equipment, but now I do so I'm actually the best person to help you.'

Now that I could see his face, I could tell that he was definitely older than me - maybe early 50s. His face had more lines than the London underground and his eyebrows were in the "crazy paedo" style, but his slumped shoulders and sadness made him look like a scared little boy.

He obviously didn't know whether he could trust me or not, because even though he'd read about me in the paper, he didn't know who the hell I was. I could be the devil for all he knew. *'Nah... I'm too pretty to be the devil.'*

He turned his head back to the water and shuffled his feet nearer the edge.

'I can do this, I can do this, I can do this, I can do thi-' He muttered repeatedly.

'No, you can't,' I said, irritated, crossing my legs and folding my arms. 'You can't do this, nor do you need to. I can help you make it a nice, dignified death rather than this rushed jumping thing you've got going on.' He continued his cowardly mutterings. 'I have to say that one of the worst things to ever happen to me was waking up in that hospital and seeing my mother's face, only to realise that I was still alive. I say one of the worst things because you can't really top what I went through as a child with an alcoholic mother, a mute father and a crazy Catholic sister.'

'Your sister is a Catholic?' he asked, turning his head back around to look at me.

'Yes, it's the shame of the family so we try not to talk about it.'

'What does the Bible say about this?' he asked, looking down at his feet.

SANDRA

What does the Bible say? Mmm, well, the Bible isn't really that keen on the old suicide thing, but there again it also isn't that keen on shellfish and mixed fabrics, so it's swings and roundabouts really.

'The Bible is ok with it really,' I lied. 'But it doesn't matter what anyone else thinks, it's what you think that matters and if you want to do this then great, but I think you should trust me and let me help you do it properly. Imagine what your life will be like if this goes wrong and you end up severely disabled.'

He looked at me out of the corner of his eye, clearly very close to giving in, judging by the look of his deeply furrowed paedo eyebrows, and by the fact that he had stopped telling himself that he could do it.

'You have to promise that you'll help me die or I'll come back and haunt you,' he said, looking at me sadly.

'I promise. I'll make it painless and easy. There'll be no need to drag your disgusting paralysed body from the river.' He turned back and stared at the water for a few minutes longer. He clearly wasn't going to jump, or he would've done it by now. Typical man, always fannying about, but I had had enough now.

'Fine, jump!' I threw my hands up in frustration, got up off the bench and walked towards my car, because as much as I would have liked to watch someone try to jump to their death on a Sunday night, I had better places to be.

'Ok, wait… I'm coming. Please don't leave me,' he croaked. I stopped walking and swivelled back around to him. He mumbled to himself as he climbed awkwardly back over the railings.

Once he had eventually got himself back onto the proper side of the railings and had stopped muttering under his breath, he stood in front of me, looking sad.

'Can you take me home, please? I only brought enough money for a one-way taxi,' he asked, wiping the mixture of rain and tears from his face.

'Fine, but no moaning about my music,' I told him. I didn't care if he was suicidal; if he complained about my reggae mix tape, then he

7

could get to fuck.

I moved the clutter off the passenger seat and we both sat in my Volvo, dripping with rain, looking out onto the deserted road ahead.

'I'm Sandra.' I said, offering my hand out. He ignored it and kept his eyes forward. 'And I thought I was bad at pleasantries,' I mumbled, dropping my hand and driving away from the curb to rejoin the road.

'I'm Graham,' he said finally. 'I live off Ingram Road.'

'Divorced?' I asked, pressing play on my tape player, which was precariously balanced on the dashboard.

'How did you guess?' Graham mumbled back, as the reggae beats started to play.

'Well, a man with your current disposition isn't likely to have a loving wife at home waiting for him. Plus, you've got the mental torment of someone who has been divorced,' I said, as I drove towards the area where I thought Ingram Road was. Even though I had lived here all my life, I'd never heard of the road.

'Yes, I'm divorced; she took the children, the money and the dog. She's allergic to the thing!' he shrieked, shaking his head in disbelief that she had taken the dog out of spite. He clearly didn't know women at all.

I wasn't good at consoling people or telling them how sorry I was to hear about their shit lives, so we just sat in awkward silence as I drove through the dark country lanes. Eventually, I stopped guessing where to go and leaned over Graham's legs, trying to get my sat nav out of the glove box.

'Six years later and I'm still depressed,' he said, out of nowhere. I eventually set the sat nav up and stuck it to the windscreen as he continued to describe how pathetic his life was.

'So, I thought I'd jump off the bridge… until you showed up.' Graham continued whining, which he seemed to enjoy. He looked at me, realising that I hadn't said anything for a while.

'I couldn't shut you up on the bridge and now you've gone mute or something!' he snapped.

'I've learnt that the less you speak the more someone else will,' I replied, not mentioning the fact that I was actually trying to listen to my favourite Jimmy Cliff song - *"I can see clearly now,"* although, somewhat ironically, the rain hadn't gone.

It was clear to me that Graham had decided to end his sadness his own way, rather than just carrying on until something else killed him. *'Good for him,'* I thought. I almost felt warm inside, knowing that I was going to help this poor man. It was a feeling so foreign to me that I didn't know whether to smile or puke.

'What's this plan of yours then?' he asked.

'I'll meet you at your place after work tomorrow and we'll do it then.'

'You're not going to shoot me, are you?'

'What? No, of course I'm not going to shoot you! Jesus...'

'So, what is this plan of yours then?' Graham asked again, clearly becoming more and more concerned about the idea.

'A painless, relaxing, zen-like suicide bag,' I told him, as I turned left onto Ingram road.

'A what?!' He shrieked loudly, making me jump. When I had Googled my friend Mary's suicide bag suggestion at lunch, I had rather liked the sound of it. Plus, it was both painless and traceless, apparently.

'Third left, the farm is at the end. What the hell is a suicide bag?!' Graham asked. I explained that a suicide bag wasn't half as scary as it seemed; in fact, it was quite romantic. And it was the only guaranteed way for me to help him, apart from shooting him in the face, but I imagined that would probably hurt like a bitch. Although, to be fair, people who get shot are always saying how they didn't realise that they'd actually been shot until years later, when they'd had an x-ray and the doctor had found a bullet wedged into their muscle.

A suicide bag is an oxygen mask or plastic bag placed over the face, which is then filled with helium through a special tube attached to a small helium tank.

'The body doesn't recognise the difference between oxygen and helium, meaning that even though the helium is essentially suffocating you, you won't realise or even feel a thing. Wonderful isn't it?' I said, sounding a bit too chirpy. Well, I thought it sounded wonderful, even if Graham didn't. It was definitely going to be my method of choice the next time I tried to kill myself.

Swaying in the fierce wind, the sign for Oakley's Farm bashed against the gate at the entrance to the 102 acres of land owned by the wet suicidal man sat on my passenger seat. I drove through the entrance and continued up the dirt track to the house, before parking up and turning off the engine.

'I'm going to help you, but I don't want to end up being finger banged by some butcho called Flick-Knife Maggie in prison. So, this has to be done a certain way, *kapish?*' Graham stared at me blankly. 'You didn't want to jump. That was clear. Of course, as it took me all of 30 minutes to talk you down, you don't want to keep on living either, but that's really none of my business. I want to help you, but you need to trust me.' I waited for a reply, but Graham just sat there, staring at me. His silent brooding was wearing very bloody thin.

'If you sod it up, I mean it, I'll come back and haunt you,' he said sadly, a small tear rolling down his face.

'Naturally. So, I'll come over tomorrow evening about 8pm and you do whatever you need to do. If you change your mind then just tell me at any time, but once we start there's no going back, okay?'

'My ex-wife isn't going to change her mind, is she?' he said, wiping the tear away.

'Well, you've got me there, Graham,' I said, holding my hands up in defeat. We sat in silence for a few moments. Graham was busy silently crying and I was busy wondering why he wasn't getting out of my car.

'Well then, I'll see you tomorrow night,' I said, looking at him and then at the passenger door, trying to tell him as politely as possible to get out, so I could go home to those bottles of Pinot and intellectual comedy.

Graham got out of the car and I watched as he slowly walked up to his house, never turning around to say goodbye. I sat in the car, staring at the house for a few moments longer, working things out in my head. The nearest neighbour was about 200 metres away, but the thick muddy driveway could be problematic if Graham's death was investigated and they found my Volvo's tyre marks. But the probability of them doing that was slim. He was depressed so he killed himself - case closed.

3

Sandra

It had been eight months since I had failed miserably to kill myself and it was finally time to put on a bra and go back to work.

I worked at Malford hospital, but no, not as a doctor. Neither was I a nurse or any other life-saving hero; I was, in fact, just the receptionist. I liked to tell people that I was just the receptionist before they had a chance to bore me stupid with stories about their suspicious lumps, peculiar moles or recent bouts of pus-filled haemorrhoids.

When the paramedics brought me in from my failed suicide attempt, I was wheeled passed my own front desk with my face covered in sick, piss down my leg and my breasts flopping about freely; a real stunner, let me tell you.

The day was to begin with the monthly staff meeting, held by German medical director and general asshat, Leonard Steinberg.

Out of the corner of my eye, I could see all the smokers outside the car park peering in to see the local celebrity, as I made my way into the safety of the temperamental lift. They didn't get a good look at me, but they knew who I was; my return to work had been splashed across the front of the Malford Herald. Somehow, the news of my suicide attempt had gotten into the local newspaper, and rumour had it that one of the underpaid nurses had sold the story. What a bitch!

The newspaper wrote the story as if I had tried to kill myself because of the recent NHS funding cuts, but that was a load of bollocks, because

I had been overworked and underpaid at the hospital for five years beforehand; the new cuts had made no difference at all.

Although the pricks at the newspaper had tried their best to reach me the day after my attempt, I was "unavailable for comment" – largely due to the fact that I was attached to hundreds of tubes while dribbling down my own chin.

Once I was out of a coma and in my own bed, I read the newspaper article and decided that I would never show my face in the hospital again. All the staff members knew and, thanks to the article, all of the patients did too. I began to think about what other types of job I could go for; maybe retail or even hospitality - you know, something to *really* make me want to kill myself.

Even if I did get an interview for another job, as soon as the interviewer Googled my name, they'd find out what I'd done.

'I can't face going back to that hospital,' I told my mother. 'Maybe I should try and get a different job.'

'No one wants a suicidal maniac in employment, darling. Well, apart from Poundland, where everyone asks you how much things are and looks at you like you're a poor skinny Polish woman,' my mother had told me during our daily "Make sure Sandra isn't dead" phone call.

It was alright for my mother to say that I should return to my job at the hospital; she wasn't the one who was about to walk into a room where everyone was sitting, thinking about my dribbling, comatose body.

Leonard had called the meeting ten minutes before I turned up in order to speak to everyone first. However, due to some late attendees, he was still halfway through his speech when I walked into the room.

'Please, can we all have some sensitivity and -' I froze in the doorway, holding the door open, not making a sound so that I could hear what else he was planning on saying. But he stopped and turned to look at me.

I looked around at my beaming colleagues, then slowly walked towards the empty chair in between Ursula, the head of midwifery, and my fellow receptionist, Scottish Mary. I called her Scottish Mary because she very sternly told me to:

'My name is Scottish Mary because I'm from Scotland and my name is Mary. Don't ever think that I'm some sort of English twat, cause I ain't, and if you *do* ever think that I'm English, I'll kick you so hard in the crotch that you'll be having a period out of your mouth!' Nice lady.

Leonard opened the meeting with the latest notices, giving Scottish Mary a chance to lean into me and whisper ridiculously loudly into my ear.

'He was just saying that we all need to be nice to you and not mention that you tried to kill yourself.' She winked at me.

'Thank you, Mary,' I whispered back, still staring straight ahead.

'By the way, you know that suicide bag thing I told you about? Well, that fat bloke from Eastenders killed himself with one at the weekend apparently… Told you all the celebs are using them!' Mary laughed, nudging me in the arm playfully.

Leonard was waffling on about the latest hospital news that a) no one cared about and b) everyone knew anyway, so I spent my time staring at the same spot on the wall behind him, which I initially thought was a blob of paint, but had now decided it looked more like a squashed mosquito.

'Psst.' Someone whispered to me from the other side of the room, causing Leonard to stop talking and look around, confused. I refused to turn around. 'Psssst!' The sound came louder and longer.

'What *is* that?' Leonard asked, as he twisted his neck around, looking at the pipes on the ceiling as if the noise was a gas leak. No one answered, and the noise stopped. 'Right, anyway… as I was saying, the number of people dying since last month has gone down but the number of life-saving operations has gone up, so let's all keep an eye on that.'

'Hey Sandi!' Rosie whispered loudly, clearly not settling for being ignored. I turned my head around slightly and saw Rosie waving madly at me. Rosie was from paediatrics and was the town bicycle - 'more cocks than a hen house' - Mary's words, not mine. 'Good to see you back!' She stuck her thumb up at me but then noticed that on that particular thumbnail, a bit of nail polish had chipped off. 'Oh, what the f-?' Rosie spent the rest of the meeting picking her nail polish off, while I spent the time counting how many legs the mosquito still had attached to its body.

'And finally, welcome back Sandra. Now, everyone back to their departments, *auf wiedersehen*, goodbye, whatever,' Leonard said flippantly, throwing his hands up in the air. With a quick smile at me, he clicked his pen closed, put it in his shirt pocket and toddled happily out of the room.

Everyone shuffled out of the staff room, while politely grinning at me like I was an unfortunate child with a cleft palate. Rosie ran off to top up her nail varnish, Scottish Mary waddled back to the reception desk and Ursula's pager bleeped as she stood up to hug me, even though she knew I hated hugs.

'Oh, crap it! Someone's about to have triplets and they're only now wanting pain relief! Bonkers. Anyway darling, I love you, welcome back and stay strong.' Ursula rubbed my arm patronisingly and slipped a card into my hand before dashing off to a woman in labour, who was by now screaming for an epidural that I imagined she had insisted she didn't want.

"I'm really glad you didn't succeed in killing yourself, welcome back!" Ursula had written in perfect calligraphy inside the card. I put the card in the bin and stuffed one of the free breakfast pastries into my mouth.

Ursula had been my friend ever since university, where she had gone to graduate with a 1st in midwifery, marry a very rich doctor and live in a huge house. I, however, had not.

Two elderly women walked passed the open staff room door and immediately recognised me from the newspaper.

'Oh, there's that nurse who tried to kill herself!' one gossiped to the other.

'What? No!' the other gasped in shock.

'I'm just the receptionist!' I replied, but they couldn't hear me, probably because they were very old and their ability to hear anything further than 2 centimetres away from their ears no longer existed.

My three-hour shift on the front desk was as boring as ever. Why was my shift just three hours? Well, quite frankly, that's none of your business. But if you must know, it's because my doctor said that I should be introduced back into my normal (fucking mundane) life slowly.

On the way back to my car, I paid a quick visit to the supply cupboard before speeding out of the staff car park to get supplies for my "special evening" with Graham.

Originally, I had thought of buying the canisters for my suicide bag from Argos, but that seemed like the stupidest fucking idea. Everyone knew everyone in Malford and if the local suicidal woman was seen buying five helium canisters from the local Argos, then everyone would know about it before I'd even left the shop.

The only thing for it was to drive just outside of Malford and buy them from a selection of different independent party shops, thereby arousing zero suspicion and supporting local businesses like an absolute hero.

Sell-A-Brate was situated in between a variety of other independent corner shops, just ten minutes from Malford town centre.

'Having a kid's birthday, are we?' the shopkeeper chirped, as she rang through the helium canister on the till.

'Yeah, it's my daughter's third birthday. She just loves balloons,' I lied through a mockingly fake smile as I handed the cash over.

'It's the little bastard's first birthday,' I told the next party shop assistant, creating a different story for every shop I went in.

'My gay friend is having a coming-out party.'

'Mum's 70th.'

'Are you having a kid's birthday party?' the last shop assistant asked.

SANDRA

'Fuck no! I'm having a porn and Pimms party!' I replied, pretending that I was insulted at the accusation that I had kids. 'Does my body look like it's carried around another human for nine months before being pushed out of my vagina?'

'God... no madam... I'm so sorry!'

'I'm joking. To be honest, yes, my body *does* look like that, but I hate kids. So no, the helium isn't for a kid's birthday party.'

'Wonderful, will you be needing any balloons?'

'What for?'

I found it amazing how much chit-chat bollocks the shop assistants were willing to partake in just to get paid minimum wage. It was meant to be minimum wage, minimum effort, wasn't it? Not minimum wage, maximum bullshit. Why couldn't I just walk into a shop, pay for an item and then fuck off without my arse being rimmed?

It was like when I went to the hairdressers. I didn't give a fuck about how long the hairdresser had been working there or when they were off to shag their way around Magaluf. I just wanted my hair to be shorter.

Now, time to pay Graham a little visit.

On my way to the farm, my soon-to-be-ex-husband had texted me to see how I was. As annoying as the twat was, he had reminded me to switch my phone off so that I couldn't be traced to the area, should any shit go down.

I laughed to myself. The last time shit went down in Malford was when I tried to kill myself; I really was the town's most notorious resident. But Oliver, the soon-to-be-ex, said he needed to talk to me about something urgently, so I naturally ignored him, I'd rather get a root canal on every tooth in my head than listen to him whine on.

Graham's farm was nearer than I had remembered and a lot bigger. By the look of the plant pots lining the fence, this place had once been looked after, but judging by the cracks, complete with dead flowers and weeds spurting out of them, they hadn't been tended to in a long time. I hid the Volvo beside the large shrubbery in the driveway and turned off the engine and my 80s disco beats.

I sat in the car and stared up at the light brown farmhouse. A small light was on in the upstairs bedroom. Was I really going to do this? Could I kill someone? Well, if I didn't kill Graham then he was going to kill himself anyway, so I wasn't really doing anything wrong here - I was just helping him do the inevitable. Plus, if I got caught, I could always try to kill myself again and with this new method. I would *definitely* die this time, so I really had nothing to lose.

Now that the morals weren't an issue, it was just the method. I knew the process inside out, but not having performed it before, I didn't know whether I could do it correctly.

As I quietly closed the car door, I suddenly had a thought that I should probably check the place out before grabbing my stuff, just in case Graham had called the police. It would be a bit suspicious if I just wandered in with a suitcase full of suicide equipment; I'd have a hard job explaining that one to the local detective.

The farm was a bit of a shithole and had clearly seen better days, but there were still a number of healthy-looking cows and sheep behind the house, grazing on the overgrown grass. I climbed the broken stairs of the front porch up to the house and knocked gently on the web-covered door. The door creaked open under the pressure of my light knocking.

'Hello?' my voice echoed as I stepped inside the house cautiously. No reply. 'Graham…' God, I hope he hasn't beaten me to it.

4

Sandra

As I walked into the old musky kitchen, I saw an envelope standing up against a vase on the table; it had "Marg" written on it. My eyes explored the pine kitchen. There were no pictures of his children or tacky ornaments from shit Spanish holidays, just a few jars of dried pasta and seeds on the windowsill. The floor was spotless, the dishes were washed and put away and the place was, apart from the thick dust that covered the skirting boards, absolutely immaculate.

I walked over to the table and reached for the envelope.

'Christ, how did you get in?!' Graham yelped, startling me slightly, as he walked into the kitchen with a newspaper under his arm and his hands still doing up his flies.

'You left the door open,' I replied, regaining my composure.

'You're early,' he mumbled, as he finished with his trousers, 'I was just having my last toilet trip; I don't want to pee myself in front of you when it happens,' Graham said, trying to muster a smile. Just a piss? I'd put money on it that he'd also taken a shit ton of laxatives as well. I'd promised him that I would let him die with dignity and it wouldn't be very dignified if he died covered in shit and piss, smelling like Satan's arsehole.

'Cup of tea?' he asked, while flapping about with the newspaper, unsure of what to do with himself, 'I'm sorry, but you need to help me because I don't know what to do here. You need to tell me what's going to happen.' Graham flapped his arms at his side like a frustrated penguin. His nervousness was making mine worse, I needed to get him to just fucking calm it.

'We're going to take this nice and slowly. I'll explain exactly what I'm going to do, and we'll just take it from there.' I gently took his arm and sat him down on the wicker chair in the corner. He began to bounce his knee up and down feverishly, as beads of sweat escaped from his forehead. 'But first, you need to just breathe in. Do it with me: big, slow breath in. Lovely… and now breathe out.' Graham let out a huge, quick sigh. 'No, you're meant to breathe out just as slowly as you breathed in. Let's do that again. Okay, breathe in, 2, 3, and out, 2, 3. Much better. Don't worry; there'll be no sudden surprises, and if you change your mind then just tell me and I'll leave.' My tone was direct as I attempted to convince him that I knew what I was doing, but naturally I didn't have a bloody clue.

Graham nodded and mopped the sweat away from his forehead with his sleeve. 'You pop up to your bedroom and put some pyjamas on, or whatever you want to wear. I'm going to get my stuff and I'll see you upstairs in a few minutes.'

Whatever Graham chose to wear would, depending on his beliefs, end up being his ghost outfit for the rest of eternity, and those piss-stained jeans and lumberjack shirt weren't exactly suitable.

He walked up the creaky staircase to his bedroom, giving me a chance to finally open the unsealed envelope on the table. I don't care if that's immoral it's not often you get to read someone's suicide note, free from emotion.

Marg,

I'm so sorry that I had to do this, but I couldn't bear to live without you anymore. Please make sure the kids don't hate me, tell them how much I love them and how I had no choice.

The farm and everything is for the kids. Please don't take any of it, you've already bled me dry once. Make sure the animals are well looked after and whatever you do, don't give them to Phil next door.

I had dreams for us Marg, I will wait for you in the afterlife. Give Rover a hug from me.

Graham

Gosh, that was more sickening that I thought it was going to be. What a sap. I held the letter in my hands for a few moments longer, thinking about the sentence, "I had dreams for us".

He didn't seem like the sentimental type, but then again, he had ended the letter with "Give Rover a hug from me," which was a bit sadistic, considering she was allergic to the dog.

It had been nearly ten minutes since Graham had gone upstairs and I'd gone back to my car, opened the boot and picked up my large suitcase containing one helium canister (the rest were under the blanket in the boot just in case), a tube, some tape, a CPAP mask, a pot of silicone gel and a large chocolate bar. The chocolate bar was for me, in case the whole thing dragged on and I got hungry.

Walking up the creaky staircase, I looked around at the rest of the house, which was furnished similarly to the kitchen; everything was pine. Even if Graham got rid of 99.9% of the pine in his house, he'd still have too much. As I approached the entrance to his bedroom, I still couldn't see any pictures of his family. Maybe his ex-wife really had taken everything.

I left the suitcase outside the room and found Graham sitting in his bedroom, combing his thinning hair in front of a black vanity table that his ex-wife clearly hadn't wanted. It was the only thing she had left behind that wasn't pine. The small bedroom was decorated with old American-themed furniture, with a double bed tucked into the corner opposite the large window that overlooked the fields, where the cows and sheep were grazing.

Graham put his comb back into the vanity table and shut the drawer slowly.

'This is the last time I'll shut this drawer,' he mumbled to himself. I turned to look at him, but had to stop myself from telling him to stop being such a sentimental little bitch. 'Come on Graham, stop being soppy. You can do this,' he said to himself.

'You can stop this right now Graham. Just say the word and I'll leave. You'll never have to see me again - well, not unless we bump into each other in a shop or something - but rest assured, I'll happily ignore you.' Even if he didn't want me to, I would ignore him anyway. I ignored everyone when I saw them in a shop; it didn't matter whether they were my colleague or my mother, I'm not a fan of conversing with people in public.

'I want to do this, I really do. It's just not as impulsive as throwing myself off that bridge...'

'This is pretty much guaranteed to work though,' I replied with a grin, trying my best to put his mind at rest.

'Pretty much? What does that mean?' Graham snapped. My face dropped. It was just a turn of phrase. One minute he's a sentimental fool, the next he's a raging old grump. No wonder his wife left him.

'It *will* work Graham, I just need you to tell me that you're still willing to do this and we'll crack right on. The longer we procrastinate, the more chance there is of you saying 'no' and then saying 'yes', then saying 'no' and then 'yes' and 'no' again. And that won't get us anywhere, so what do you want?' I said, a bit too sternly for a man who was clearly feeling a bit fragile.

'I still want you to help me kill myself,' he mumbled sadly.

'Excellent, now what I need you to do for me, Graham, is get into bed and sit yourself up against this lovely headboard,' I instructed, matter-of-factly, while plumping the pillows and propping them up against the wicker headboard.

He got up slowly and walked around to his bed, which I had turned down for him like some sort of hotel cleaner. He slipped his legs in between the cold, crisp sheets. 'Do you know what's funny?' he said, with the tiniest hint of a smile. 'I went online and visited some suicide forums trying to find someone to help me, and nobody replied. So, I went to the bridge to do it myself and then you turn up. Funny isn't it?' he said, a tiny laugh escaping from his mouth. I wouldn't call it funny, I'd call it ridiculously ironic. But what the hell was this suicide forum thing he was talking about? I'd have to Google that shit later - after I'd finished with Graham of course.

I wheeled my suitcase into the room, whacked it at the bottom of the bed and opened it up. I began taking the items out one by one. First the helium canister, then the long tube with the CPAP mask attached.

Graham frowned at the apparatus that I had just got out of my case and put in front of him.

'What the hell is *that*?!' he shrieked, pointing at the helium canister with pure terror. I wasn't sure why he was so shocked to see the canister; how else did he think I was going to bring the helium? In a big bunch of sodding unicorn balloons?

'It's a helium canister Graham. It's the main component of this whole thing, along with the tubing and the full-face CPAP mask and all the other bits. Remember the nicely nicknamed suicide bag I was telling you about? Well… Voilà!' I said, pointing at the thing in all its glory.

I went on to explain the procedure that I was about to carry out. I'd put the gel around his nose and mouth, then the CPAP mask would be placed over his face, the tubing would be attached to the mask and to the helium canister, I'd then turn it on and Bob's your uncle, Fanny's your aunt, we have ourselves a killer suicide bag.

I also mentioned that I wasn't 100% sure how much helium he'd need, but I told him not to worry because I had another four canisters as backup.

'Where are the other canisters?' he said, looking out into the hallway to see if there were more suitcases waiting to be brought in.

'They're in my boot. I'll start, then go down and get them if and when they are needed.' I clapped my hands together, signalling that I was ready to hurry this thing along.

Graham sat up in bed, frowning even harder at the items in front of him.

'This is a painless and easy way to go. I promise you. Sleeping tablets aren't guaranteed and I can't get my hands on anything else, other than things that are going to put you through a lot of pain. Trust me.'

'I meant it you know,' Graham said.

'What?'

'If you fuck it up, I'll come back and haunt you.'

'Understandably. If I fuck it up, which I won't, then when you do actually die, you can come back and haunt me all you like.'

'Ok.' Graham took a deep breath and let out a big, slow sigh. I'd taught him well.

'So, who's going to find you?' I asked.

'The cleaner,' he answered without looking at me.

'Charming. Wait, you have a cleaner?'

'Yes, why are you so surprised?'

'Because your house is filthy.'

'Yeah, I guess it is. She's more of a thief than a cleaner, I'm sure she'll clean me out of anything of any worth before she calls someone.'

'Only if she likes pine,' I replied with a smile, but Graham just looked at me, confused.

'When you're ready Graham, I'll begin.' He shuffled slightly under the covers and nodded to me to go ahead.

I put the cold silicone gel around the edges of Graham's nose and mouth to ensure that the CPAP mask didn't leave any marks for the coroner to find. The mask was then secured over his head and placed over his mouth and nose, with the tube tightly secured at the opening.

I slowly and carefully turned the valve on the canister.

'Is it on?' he mumbled through the mask.

'I think so.' I leaned into the valve and heard the tiny hissing flow of helium. 'Yes, it's on. Now we wait,' I said to him, checking to see if there were any holes in the tube and mask connection. There weren't, so I went and sat on the stool and stared at Graham, who looked quite funny with all the apparatus on.

Now I just had to wait for him to fall unconscious and die. Not so difficult. I was surprised that a) it had been pretty easy so far and b) I didn't feel bad or guilty about what I was doing. Maybe that was because Graham was a bit of a twat. Obviously, it's not a sin to be a bit of a twat, but my soon-to-be-ex-husband is a twat and if I could help him on his way off this mortal coil, then I very much would.

Graham turned away from me and turned his head to look out of the window and down onto his farm. The darkness covered most of the fields, but the outside light mixed itself in with the moonlight, creating a glow just bright enough for us to see the fields and a particularly fat cow, munching on the overgrown grass.

I watched the cow chew the grass, in awe of the simplicity of her life; chew, poo, chew, poo, die, Wetherspoons burger meal deal, digested, plopped out into the toilet. Done. No need to be content with life, no knowledge of how cuntish people are and no soon-to-be-ex-husband texting you every five fucking minutes. What a dream.

'I put my watches in the freezer,' Graham muttered slowly, his last words as he gradually slipped into unconsciousness. Either the helium had made him delirious, or he had *actually* put his watches in the freezer. Either way, I didn't care enough to go and find out.

Fifty minutes had passed since I had first turned the helium nozzle, so I gave him a nudge. There was no response, so I punched him hard on the arm. Nothing. Graham's head had slumped forward slightly over his chest. One last thump, still nothing. Christ, that was bloody quick! I didn't even get around to eating my chocolate bar.

After gently pulling the mask off of his face, I felt for a pulse. There was none. I put my ear over his mouth to check for any signs of breathing - again, nothing. He was definitely dead. Awesome.

I stood at the bottom of the bed and looked out of the window, taking in the moonlit view for a few moments. The fat cow from earlier stared up at me while chewing slowly on a tuft of grass. I grabbed both curtains and pulled them abruptly together. I didn't want some fat fucking cow giving me a judgmental stare.

5

Roddy

Dom, Malford's lowest ranking police officer and the medic whose name I can never remember, were sat at the kitchen table when I walked into the farmhouse. I'd had a rather annoying phone call from Dom. He'd told me that some cleaning bird had found her boss dead in his bed and that I had to attend. I hadn't even had my second breakfast yet and I was already out in the community solving crimes, which to be honest, had made me even more hungry.

The McDonald's drive-thru had been too busy to queue at, so I'd had to forget about my stomach and drive straight to Graham's. I wasn't happy, but I was Detective Inspector Benjamin Roddy of Malford and people had very high expectations of me.

'Right, what's all this nonsense about?' I asked, stepping into the farmhouse with my muddy boots.

'The cleaner found him dead in his bed when she turned up to her cleaning shift this morning. After she found him cold and stiff, it would seem that she stuffed her bags full of his most expensive possessions too, as we found a couple of bottles of aftershave and an expensive looking shampoo in her handbag,' Dom said, raising a judgemental eyebrow to the cleaner, who was next to him, smoking a cigarette.

'I told them that it was too late for a medic as the farmer was already colder than a witch's titty on a brass broomstick,' the cleaner told me in an accent that was hard for me to understand, but I sort of got the gist of it. She had said something about someone having a witch's titty and an ass broomstick.

'So, you didn't try to resuscitate him?' I barked at the cleaner, who was chewing her gum in between cigarette drags like a retarded horse.

'No, he was already dead. I know my kisses are good but they're not good enough to resurrect old dirty farmers,' the cleaner replied, as she dabbed her ash on the floor.

When suicides were reported to us at Malford police station, even if they weren't suspicious, the lowest ranking police officer, Dom, was sent to the scene so he could write up a report. The report would then be filed in the "suicides and closed cases" drawer back at the station, which currently contained four cases. One was from some American bloke, then a failed attempt from one of his daughters and two from a suicide pact back in the 60s involving two queer blokes who were going to be chemically castrated.

The very few suicides that had occurred in Malford hadn't been investigated, because I didn't believe in wasting taxpayers' money on lowlifes who were dead anyway.

Everyone and their dog in Malford knew that I was the best detective in the area and that if there was a real crime - which there never was - then I would be the one to solve it. If it was a boring crime, then Dom would attend. Although saying that, Dom had once told me that I was a useful as a ham sandwich at a Bar Mitzvah, but I didn't understand what that meant - unless it was something to do with the club sandwich that I had been eating at the time.

'There's no clear sign of suicide boss,' Dom said.

'Is that a suicide note?' I pointed to the letter and empty envelope on the table.

'Yes, this is a suicide note, but there's no visible cause of death and having gone through the bins, it doesn't seem like he used anything to kill himself. In fact, it looks more like a murder that's been set up as a suicide. That's why we had to disturb you, boss,' Dom replied, looking sheepishly at my muddy boots.

I had joined the police force at the tender age of 18 and had made detective 12 months later because I was sharp, excellent at investigating crimes and a great police officer. Definitely not because there was no one else to fill the role.

'Roddy, you've made detective. Don't call me,' the Chief Inspector had told me, as he walked out of the police station on the way to the Costa del Semi-Retirement.

The cleaner asked me whether she was still going to get paid or not.

'Have you done any cleaning this morning?' I laughed, looking at the state of the dust everywhere.

'No, I'm not going to dust a dead guy's house, am I?' she replied, throwing her cigarette into a glass of water on the table.

'Then you're not going to get paid. are ya?' I said, using the same teenage tone that she had used. The stupid bint got up, threw her handbag over her shoulder and stormed towards the door.

'Er, excuse me.' I stopped her in her tracks. She turned and gave me an evil look.

'What?'

'Your pockets.' I pointed towards her coat pockets. She rolled her eyes and took out a hand full of silver cutlery, throwing it on the table with a loud clang.

'Eres un estúpido policía gordo con un pene pequeño!' she snapped, as she stormed out of the house, slamming the door behind her.

'Ah German, such a lovely language,' I said, checking out the cutlery before throwing it in the sink.

'Great, now she's gone we can do some proper police work. This had better be good and quick because Holly and Phil are doing a bit on This Morning about a bloke with two penises and I don't want to miss it. Anything in here for breakfast?' I asked, as I walked over to the fridge and opened it up. A solitary jar of mayo sat on the shelf. The freezer, however, had a mountain of men's watches and a wad of notes stashed in it. 'Hmmm... man puts money and jewellery in the freezer... Did he have dementia?'

The medic explained that Graham's medical records showed that he had been diagnosed with depression.

'And would that cause him to put his valuables in the freezer?' Dom asked. The medic told him that it would not.

'Maybe he was hiding it from sticky fingers out there,' I suggested, raising my eyebrows at the cleaner outside the kitchen window, who was busy lighting up another cigarette.

'¿Por qué no vas y te follas?' the cleaner shouted through the closed door.

'That's what I thought,' I said, as I picked up the letter and read it, hoping to find the answer. 'Nope, still doesn't explain the frozen watches. Right, let's take a look at the dead guy.' The three of us went up the creaky stairs to the bedroom, where Dom and the medic informed me about what they had concluded, which was a fat load of nothing.

I half listened to what the two were saying to me while I nosed around the room, amazed at how much pine there was. Then I spotted the cows.

'Oh look, he's got cows! I love cows.'

'Of course, we won't know the actual cause of death until a post-mortem is carried out,' the medic explained, but I wasn't really listening as I was too busy counting how many cows there were in the field. He went on for a bit longer and I planned to start listening properly once I'd counted the cows, but he stopped abruptly before I had the chance.

'Very good, very good,' I said, spinning around from the window. There were 18 cows in the field.

'What is, Sir?' the medic asked with his arms crossed, clearly not impressed with me not listening.

'What you just said. We'll do the post-mortem, see what that says and if it doesn't say that he died of natural causes, then maybe I'll investigate further. You, lower ranking police officer-'

'My name is Dom, I've worked with you for five years,' he said.

'Who? Yes, well, I need you to secure the scene, get forensics, get the coroner to take his body and I'll head back to the station.' Dom had only dealt with a dead body at a crime scene three times before. This actually meant that he was already a lot more experienced than I was, but I wasn't going to tell him that. He'd start getting too big for his boots and the police station wasn't big enough for two alpha males.

I drove back to the station but was very annoyed after discovering that I'd missed the McDonald's breakfast. I had to settle for two Big Mac meals instead. Today really had got off to the worst possible start.

It got even worse when I arrived back at the station to find the Chief Inspector on his annual visit. He was busy rummaging through the files that had been abandoned on my desk, when I walked into the station midway through swallowing a handful of fries.

'Rodders!' the Chief shouted, even though he was only standing a few feet away from me. 'What's all this about a suicide?'

'Well, we're not sure that it *is* a suicide actually-' I replied, trying to swallow the clump of fries without choking.

'Not a suicide?! You mean we could have a Malford murderer on the loose?!' he shouted.

'Not quite, Chief.'

I explained what I had found at the farm, excluding the jewellery in the freezer, and told him that I would probably need to investigate.

'There was a stupid cleaning bird at the scene. She was the one that found him, so I'd put money on it being her.'

'A cleaning bird?' the Chief questioned.

'Yeah, you know, a house cleaner. I think she was Spanish or something, tried nicking some crockery so there's definitely something dodgy going on there.'

'It's going to be a really big investigation, a really huge one. I think we should get another bobby to help me catch this cold-hearted killer,' I said, with a furrowed brow and a pretend look of concern on my face. I wanted another colleague to have some fun with and do the work for me. The only other police officer in the station was Dom and he was as fun as he was good-looking. And God, was he ugly.

'I thought you just said that it was the cleaning bird?' the Chief replied.

'No, I didn't mean she actually killed him, I meant she's probably involved-'

'We're obviously going to need some more men on the job for a case this big,' the Chief said, making it sound like it was his own decision, 'Hmm, but we don't have any money. I know! You and Dom will just have to work harder.' And with that, he flung open the doors and disappeared, leaving me with the possibility of a huge murder case and severe indigestion.

6

Sandra

The morning after dealing with Graham, I put the used helium canister in the big bins behind the block of flats and the other ones in my bath. I hardly ever had any visitors and I hardly ever bathe, so it was safe to say that no one would find them. But now I wondered what the fuck I would do with the rest of the helium. Could I do it again? Yes, that's not even a reasonable question, of course I could. I had felt a real sense of achievement helping Graham snuff it and to think I was usually just a cold-hearted bitch who rarely achieved anything other than getting drunk in front of the TV!

Perhaps this was going to be my new calling. The only issue was that I had no idea how I would find my next victim. Actually no… "victim" sounds quite negative, like I'm forcing something on them against their will, which I'm not. I'll call them "patients" instead. So, how was I going to get my next patient?

I could hang around Malford bridge and wait for the next suicidal sucker to appear, but that could take years - it really is quite a small town. There are those Samaritan posters at the end of the train station platform. I could scribble one myself, maybe put my number underneath a drawing of a paralysed quadriplegic who failed at suicide. That would encourage anyone to call me before they messed up their own attempts.

Other things that I had briefly considered included social media advertising, flyering near suicide hotspots and going into a Wetherspoons during the day; those places are full of people just waiting to die.

Obviously, I wasn't going to suddenly start being some sort of suicide hero, but I would definitely visit the suicide forum that Graham had mentioned, to see if there was any demand for my services.

My mother Janice had been staying at my sister Felicity's house to see her ugly grandchildren for two weeks; even though she loved spending time with them, it was rather cutting into her drinking time. My sister is also a big Catholic, not a hereditary condition, which rather interfered with Mother's usual wild self. So, when I agreed to meet them both she was rather relieved to finally have an excuse to be around another adult who wasn't going to tell her off for yelling "Jesus Christ!" every time her cigarette ash fell on the floor.

I walked into the coffee shop and found my mum and sister sat by the window, with three green teas that Felicity had already ordered for us.

'Actually, I'm more in the mood for a cup of cyanide,' I said as I sat down, already in the mood for an argument.

'That's stupid. Anyway, green tea is better than the vanilla latte you normally order, which is just full of sugar may I add,' Felicity said.

'No, you may not add. And also, that's exactly why I'm about to order one - one big-ass cup of diabetes please.' I gave my unimpressed mother a kiss on the cheek as she rolled her eyes and mumbled "Here we go again," under her breath. Her two daughters were both so different and she had always blamed it on our American father, James.

Our mother had said that he had treated us differently; he had treated me like I was his pride and joy and Felicity like the accidental second child that she was.

After ordering a vanilla latte and a large chocolate muffin (just to annoy Felicity), I sat and listened to how my perfect niece and nephew were getting on at their new Catholic grammar school.

'Chelsea also has her bible graduation on Sunday,' Felicity said, leaning forward and raising her eyebrows. I knew that she was expecting some sort of reply, but I couldn't give a fuck. The Bible was full of bollocks and grammar schools were elitist organisations, so anything that I wanted to say wouldn't be particularly helpful. Also, she hadn't bothered to ask how my return to work had gone.

'Gosh, I'm *so* happy for you. Oh, and my return to work went fine - thank you,' I replied, taking a sip of my extra sugary latte that was far too sugary in all honesty, but pouring the four extra sachets into it was worth the look on Felicity's face. Felicity sat back and shrugged her shoulders; she had never talked to me about my attempted suicide, and with her arms crossed even tighter and her mouth pouting like she was a teenager taking a selfie, she clearly didn't want to break the habit now.

You could put Felicity and me in a "guess which two are sisters" lineup made of three women and you would never pick the two of us out. Felicity's blonde hair was short, curly and full of mousse, whereas I had shoulder-length brown messy hair, with zero product in.

Felicity and our mother were also very different; Felicity wore a necklace with a cross on it, whereas Mother's jewellery of choice was a ton of brightly-coloured gay rainbow bracelets. In fact, my parents should've done a DNA test to check whether Felicity was definitely their biological offspring or just some religious intruder. I really hoped that she was the latter, but it was more likely to be the former; she shared my stubbornness, my hatred of other people and my short fuse when it came to our mother.

'Well, Miguel and I have some big news,' Mother piped up, excitedly clapping her hands and bouncing on her chair. Big news! Great, well she couldn't be emigrating because she'd already done that, and she couldn't be pregnant because she'd already gone through the change. Wait, had she gone through the change yet? Oh God, *please* don't be fucking pregnant.

Maybe they were getting a divorce or moving back to the UK - that would be much worse than having a new baby sibling. Oh God, please be pregnant. Mother sat on the edge of her seat, bouncing her knees up and down, looking from me to Felicity and waiting for one of us to ask her what it was. Felicity nibbled on her egg and spinach pot of protein shit and I took a massive bite out of my muffin. 'Is anyone going to ask Mummy what it is?'

'We don't call you Mummy,' Felicity and I said in unison, our mouths full.

She ignored us and told us that she and Miguel were going on a new journey of discovery; they were going to be "nun-exclusive".

'Non-exclusive,' I corrected her.

'But you're married,' Felicity said slowly, as if speaking to a stupid child.

'I'm also in my sexual prime!' Mother said, flicking her long, dyed hair over her shoulder like she was in some perfume advert, rather than an overpriced coffee shop in Malford.

Felicity, being a Catholic had never approved of our mother's lifestyle, especially when she was having an affair behind our father's back. But to be fair, Mum did promise that Dad never found out, or at least she'd said it definitely wasn't that that had made him kill himself.

His suicide was bloody good timing though, because it meant that Mother could finally be with the young sexy waiter from Mucho, the local Tapas bar, and not feel an ounce of guilt, while also getting all the inheritance money.

Poor Felicity wasn't sure at the time whether to be more annoyed at our mum or our dad; she had run off with some young bloke but he had committed suicide on her birthday. To sinfully kill yourself was one thing, but to do it on your daughter's birthday was unforgivable in Felicity's eyes.

'Isn't God all about forgiveness?' I had asked her.

'No, that's Christians. I'm Catholic, we're all about hate,' she had snapped back sarcastically, but it had been the truest thing that she had ever said. Great, now our mother was going to be putting it about everywhere. Why couldn't she be a good Catholic woman; the one

Felicity had always dreamed of?

'So, Miguel and I have been going *el speed dating*,' Mother said, clicking her fingers like a retarded flamenco dancer.

'And how does Miguel feel about this?' I asked, pretending to be interested. I had no real feelings towards my "stepdad" (who was one year younger than me); he didn't speak much English and was a bit short, but I didn't judge him solely on that. He deserved an award for putting up with our mother. When Dad killed himself, Mum and Miguel had quickly planned their wedding, but then Mum had a bit of a meltdown, or an *attack of conscience* as I call it, and she had started drinking even earlier than her usual 11am.

'You're not serious, Mum? You've only been married for a month! You can't be non-exclusive with your husband!' Felicity cried out, putting her head in her hands in desperation.

'Of course I can darling; it's the 20th-'

'21st.' I corrected her.

'-century. Us women can do what we want now! Also, I'm not getting any younger.'

'Of course you're not getting any younger! No one gets younger - that's the ultimate essence of life: *everything* gets older!' Felicity snapped at her.

'Also, it's great dating at my age because it means that you don't have to meet the parents.' Mum downed the rest of her tea and took my hands over the table, something she had never done before and something she'd never be doing again. 'But we need to talk about Sandra.'

'No we *don't*,' I said, pulling my hands away and grabbing my muffin. If my hands were busy they couldn't be held and if my mouth was full of muffin then I couldn't speak.

'You're not well though, dear. Mummy wants to know that you won't ever do it again. You won't will you?' she urged, grabbing my hand with the muffin in it and rubbing her thumb over my knuckles.

I pulled my hand away again and hid it under the table. I was fine,

SANDRA

kind of. Ok, I wasn't fine, but drunken Mummy and Miss Perfect Catholic Bint over there were the last two people I wanted to talk to about it. They both knew that me finding Dad swinging in the garage had been the main reason I had tried to overdose.

'I know you don't want to talk to us about it-' Mum began.

'Because you know what you did was wrong,' Felicity muttered under her breath.

'Well, I didn't think I'd have to deal with the aftermath if I'm being completely fucking honest!' I snapped at her; although we were both grown-ass adults, we still despised each other like we were hormonal teenage bitches.

'I just want you to promise that you won't do it again,' Mum said calmly, as she nudged Felicity and shot her an evil look.

'She's right, we don't want to lose you,' Felicity said as nicely as she possibly could, before whispering; '-even if you are a sinner,' which I ignored, like I did most stupid comments that came out of her childish mouth.

'I'm not going to do it again,' I said eventually, which Mum accepted straight away.

'Great!' Mum said, with a little hand clap. 'Right girls, I'm off to meet David,' she said, as she got up, slung her bag over her shoulder and took her coat off the back of her chair.

'Who's David?' I asked, immediately regretting it when I saw her smile sexily at her phone.

'I dunno, but this app tells me he's half a mile away.'

'*Please* mother.' Felicity begged her to stop talking.

'I'll tell you all about my adventures when you come over to Spain.'

'When we what?' Felicity and I asked in unison.

'You're coming over to Spain in a few weeks' time to spread Daddy's ashes. You haven't forgotten, have you dears? Although I'm sure he'd be happy if we just chucked them in the stinky river here, he always hated Spain - said it reminded him of when he was in the war in Vietnam. Fuck knows why. Anyway, goodbye my darling children.

Don't do anything I wouldn't!'

She swanned out of the coffee shop with her large faux fur coat slung over her shoulder. Off to shag some guy called David! I, on the other hand, was off to sign up to some suicide forums.

7

Roddy

What do I, Detective Inspector Benjamin Roddy, love more than locking up criminals? Well, nothing actually, but Scottish Mary comes a close second. She might be one of those *lesbians,* but she's the most beautiful and sweet-hearted piece of ass I've ever met. Unfortunately, though, she does happen to be the number one enemy of my pub quiz team. She always wins and is never very nice about it; she constantly gloats that she's got over 50 of the £1 mini trophies that they give to the winners.

I first set eyes on the beautiful creature that was Mary when she started at the quiz almost a year ago; I had invited her to join my team, but she had told me to "fuck off and die", which I have to admit was not the response I was looking for.

'Good evening Mary, you're looking gorgeous this evening,' I said as I walked over to her table in the pub.

'Didn't I tell you to fuck off?' she replied in her dreamy Glaswegian accent, without turning her head to look at me. 'I know your game pal, trying to sweet talk me so that I'll let you win the quiz. You can get tae fuck mate. This girl is on a winning streak and she ain't getting blindsided by the village arsehole.'

You would've thought that words like that would put me right off her, but they'd had quite the opposite effect. Her quick wit and potty mouth made my dick semi-hard. Most birds wouldn't have the balls to speak to me like that because they know what they'd get, but Mary spoke to me in a way that let me know that she was interested, sexually.

'I'm sorry Mary, I didn't mean to push your buttons,' I said, winking at her cheekily.

'The only buttons you've been pressing are the ones on your TV remote, fatty,' Mary quipped back.

'Maybe I can buy you some flowers? What's your favourite flower?'

'Self-raising,' she replied, without making eye contact. Another witty comeback! God, she should be on the stage, or in my bed. But then again, I wouldn't want her to make witty remarks about my cock.

'Maybe I can buy you a drink then?' I asked, nervously waiting for her rejection. Instead though, she turned her body around and looked up at me.

'You know what, Benny boy, that would be cracking. I'll have four pints of Carling.' She turned back round to prepare her quiz sheets.

When I returned, struggling with her four pints of lager, she said thanks and told me to fuck off back to my own table. I did, but with my head held high, because I had just bought the most beautiful bird in the pub not one, but *four* drinks.

The next morning, I had a mighty fine breakfast from the local café and made my way to the station to properly start on the dead farmer case. Unfortunately, Dom was already sitting at my desk going through the case file when I arrived with two McDonald's breakfasts.

'You brought breakfast! I'm famished!' Dom chirped when he saw my haul.

'Well, you'll have to sod off down to McDonald's then, 'cause these are mine.'

'While you eat your food, I'll inform you with what I've discovered so far, shall I?' Dom asked me, like a scared little kitten. I nodded and rolled my eyes. It wasn't even half nine and I was done with his timidity already.

'Excellent!' he beamed. 'Well, from the doctor's records it looks like our farmer was depressed-'

'Of course he was, he's a farmer! How many happy farmers do you know?'

'Quite a few actually.'

'Of course you do.'

'Well, there's Jim-'

'Is that it?'

'No, I know a few more-'

'No, I meant is that all you've found out so far, that the old git was depressed?'

'Oh I see... no, I also discovered that he's divorced...' I yawned loudly. 'Apparently it was a messy divorce, because the solicitors' files are huge and she took the kids and the dog.'

'The dog!' I said, mockingly surprised. 'Well, she *is* a spiteful bitch, isn't she? Taking a man's best friend like that. We'll need to drag her in for questioning.'

'Yes boss,' Dom said, scribbling something down on his notepad. 'And that's all I've got so far...'

'That's it?'

'Yes boss, although I haven't actually had time to go through his laptop and internet history yet.'

'Brilliant, my favourite part of the job. I'll do that, now bugger off and get yourself some breakfast.'

Dom sheepishly got up and left the station. I threw all of the files that he had put on my desk in the bin and plonked the laptop on the desk. Now, time to find the juicy stuff.

8

Sandra

Graham's death was already in the local paper; those journalist bastards didn't miss a thing. It had only been two days since they'd found him and the paper had the headline "FARMER FOUND DEAD IN SUSPICIOUS CIRCUMSTANCES" splashed across the front page in massive letters.

I didn't know what about it was suspicious, unless they were referring to the ridiculous amount of pine in his house. Further into the article, it stated that the police were investigating, and a post mortem was going to be performed to determine the cause of death. Why the fuck did they need to do that? Wasn't it obvious that he was depressed and committed suici- Ah… Thinking about it now, it might have looked a bit suspicious, there not being any sign of the actual suicide at all, apart from the note of course.

In future, I needed to set the scene afterwards to look like a more convincing suicide. Everything is trial and error the first time, isn't it? Whether it's raising kids, laying patio stones or helping the local farmer kill himself, no one knows it all before they start.

Now that I had cleared that up, I sat on my bed with my laptop open and browsed some suicide forums using a VPN to hide my IP address. I was fully *incognito* as I signed up to hangoninthere.com using the screen name "DixieDeath5000". To begin with, I didn't have a fucking clue what to write. I thought of "Dear Forum Users, Is anyone looking for some help shuffling off this mortal coil? Fantastic, please send your business my way." But then I thought that that was probably a really fucking stupid idea, not to mention in total violation of the forum rules.

Half an hour had passed and I had read through a load of comments, ranging from people asking others to refrain from killing themselves, to people telling each other to get a grip because "It's not like you're starving in Africa or infected with AIDS." True, but I doubt the starving, AIDS-ridden Africans wanted to live in Malford.

To be honest, most of the people on the forum seemed to be in the mood for trolling others, rather than killing themselves. Maybe I should do everyone a favour and just target the trolls.

Eventually, I came across a particularly interesting thread that only had one post in it; someone with the username "m0th3r_0f_drag0ns666" had asked what everyone thought about euthanasia and assisted suicide. I'm going to be honest with you - I didn't really know what the fuck I was doing on a suicide forum... well, I knew what I was *doing*; I was trying to pick up some new patients, but I didn't know how to ask someone if they might want me to help them.

The spiel that I used on Graham could work again, but I would have to tailor it a bit to make it more personal; there's nothing more irritating than when someone sends the same generic bollocks to everyone.

What I decided to do was "like" a few of the user's posts and add my own comment to the thread, with something along the lines of, "I wish that I had had someone to help me commit suicide so that I hadn't messed it up, but how do you ask someone to help you, without them trying to stop you?"

Even though I was on the lookout for another patient, I was still unsure about whether or not I was actually going to perform any more assisted suicides; on the one hand, it was illegal; on the other, it gave me a purpose until I killed myself again, so it was swings and roundabouts really.

    Two minutes later, my laptop pinged loudly at me. The Mother of Dragons had replied.

9

Roddy

The coroner met me at the entrance of his facility. It was so white that it looked 100 times more clinical than a doctor's waiting room, but with fewer girly magazines. I shook his hand hard and tried my best not to mention how un-coroner-like he looked; he was tall, black and very athletic, which was not what coroners off the telly looked like. They were normally fit blonde birds or white Irish men; well, they were in Silent Witness.

'I'm Femi, nice to meet you,' he said in a strong accent that I couldn't place. I guessed it was from somewhere in Africa because he was black - not that I'm a racist, no one in the UK police force is racist, but it's odd to see a black guy working in a such a high-profile job.

'Detective Inspector Roddy, but you can call me Roddy,' I said, with my chest puffed out, staring at Femi's rock-hard biceps as they tried desperately to burst out of his white coroner coat. I bet he had a huge dick as well.

We walked down the steel-covered corridor; steel doors, steel shelves and steel flooring.

'Have you been to a post-mortem before?' Femi asked politely, opening the large steel door for me. Lifting my head up high and strutting through the door with my hands in my pockets, I tried my very best to assert my dominance. I didn't want this Femidom bloke thinking that he was in charge here.

'Not in person, but I've seen a lot of footage,' I said casually, not mentioning that the "footage" was actually a mixture of Silent Witness, Taggart and DCI Banks.

'Excellent, you should be fine today then,' Femi replied. Unfortunately, I had a sneaking suspicion that I wasn't going to be fine and that today was going to be something of a struggle.

He closed the large steel door behind us and walked into the cutting room, a smallish room with metal wash basins on the back wall, multiple cabinets scattered around and a steel table in the middle with a dead bloke on it.

'Oh wow, you don't keep him covered up then?' I said, referring to Graham, who was laid out naked on the table, with his *fandango* out for all to see.

'No, Detective Inspector, we cannot cut him open with the sheet still over him,' Femi replied in a tone that I wasn't sure was sarcastic or not.

'Can I get you anything before we get started, Roddy?' Femi asked, with a large friendly smile on his face and his hands clasped together. I looked from Femi to the new person who had just entered the room covered in scrubs and a face mask.

I cleared my throat and tried to calm myself as Femi asked me again if he could get me anything. *"Breathe in, breathe out."* I told Femi that I didn't need anything, unless there were any milkshakes or biscuits.

'Milkshakes? No, I'm afraid we only have hot drinks. Or water.'
'Hot chocolate?'
'Afraid not.'
'Tea then, please.'
'Sugar?'
'9.'

'I'm Detective Inspector Roddy,' I said to the new woman, with my hand held out. She took one look at my hand and raised her eyebrows.

'I'm the pathologist,' she replied, turning around to prepare her instruments on the small mobile table next to Graham.

'Talkative bitch,' I muttered to myself.

'Excuse me?' she said, abruptly lowering the extendable light that they had in dentist surgeries.

'Pardon?'

'Did you say something, Inspector?'

'Nothing at all darling.' I winked at her playfully.

Femi returned with a large mug of tea and zero biscuits. I was going to complain, but then suddenly, the pathologist started her first incision and Femi got his camera out and started taking photos of Graham.

When the scalpel slit open the chest in a Y-shaped incision, I closed my eyes tightly, trying to imagine that I was just an actor in a show and the skin being cut was just some leather handbag. A leather handbag with actual organs, veins and a rather hairy, saggy scrotum.

It was when the pathologist peeled back Graham's chest skin and muscle to remove the ribcage and ligaments that I really felt sick. I took some chewing gum out of my pocket and popped it into my mouth, trying to get rid of the smell and my overwhelming urge to puke.

Each organ was examined and weighed before the pathologist began cutting from behind Graham's ear, across his forehead and over to the other ear. When the electric saw came to life, I opened my eyes widely with a mixture of excitement and pure fear.

'I'm about to see my first noggin,' I said, rubbing my hands in anticipation. Femi just stared at me.

'You're doing a great job love,' I said to the pathologist, giving her a thumbs up and some encouragement before she took the brain out, but she just stared at me as well.

'Jeez, what's up with her?' I whispered to Femi and nudged him playfully.

'Femi, I'm going to need some help here,' the pathologist said, which made Femi spring into action.

The whole thing was taking so bloody long that my chewing gum was getting stale, so when no one was looking, I took it out and popped it into the bin next to me.

After about ten minutes of the two of them fannying about, the brain was finally ready to come out. The pathologist had both hands around it as she gently lifted it out of the skull, while Femi took some more photos.

'Well, fuck me sideways!' I blurted out involuntarily. They both froze and looked at each other for a moment, before continuing with the brain extraction.

'Excuse me, Inspector!' the pathologist shouted suddenly, making me jump and clench my buttocks hard.

'What?' I shrieked.

'Can you take your gum out of the brain basin please?' she said, staring at my gum in the small metal bin.

'Brain basin?'

'Yes, the brain basin.'

'So, it's not a bin then?'

'No.'

'Ah… Sorry,' I said, taking my gum out and popping it into the actual bin that Femi was lifting up for me.

I looked at Femi for some brotherly support, but it was difficult to read his expression, probably because I wasn't used to reading the expressions of black people.

'Birds, ay?' I laughed, nudging him in the side again.

'Could you stop nudging me please,' he replied, moving away slightly.

'Oh yeah, sorry mate,' I said, holding my hands up in apology. 'She was a bit harsh with the old chewing gum thing though, weren't she?' I whispered.

'Was she?'

'Probably bleeding, if you know what I mean.'

'Starved of oxygen,' the pathologist said out loud.

'Are you?' I asked.

'Same as the lungs then?' Femi replied.

'Seems so, but there are no marks on the face or neck to suggest strangulation.'

'Well, how else do you get starved of oxygen?' I interrupted.

10

Sandra

The Mother of Dragons had texted, me asking what I knew about assisted suicide and why had I given them my number. I replied with my own set of questions: why did they want to know about assisted suicide and did they know someone who had done it?

They replied saying; "Don't know anyone who has done it, just want some help." I had to read the text a few times before deciding that I had nothing to lose by offering my services; they didn't know who I was and there was no way to trace my second-hand pay-as-you-go mobile, so if they were trying to trap me, it wouldn't work - unless of course I turned up at their place to do the deed and they had the police waiting for me. That might be a bit of a trap.

We had been texting for a while, going back and forth about why we both thought that living was pointless and what our thoughts were on euthanasia - the usual icebreakers. We shared a few personal details (all of mine being completely made up bollocks); I won't bore you with the details, but the Mother of Dragons turned out to be a 53-year-old guy from Basingstoke with severe depression, bipolar and zero courage to do anything about it.

Eventually, I took the risk and asked him outright if he wanted me to help him. The Mother, or should I say the Father of Dragons, took his sweet time to respond but when he did he said that he would like me to, after which I went on to explain, very briefly, how I would do it. Then we arranged a date.

Later, after trying to convince Mary that she didn't have to come to Spain with me in a few weeks to scatter my father's ashes, I spotted a familiar face walking through the hospital doors.

'Don't,' Irish Jenny said, before I even had a chance to say hello. It had only been just over a week since she had last come in.

'Christ, I do like you Sandra, but I long for the day when I don't have to see you,' Irish Jenny said, plonking her bag and coat on the desk. I called her Irish Jenny because she was Irish... and her name was... you get the idea. I just assumed that, rather like Mary, she wouldn't want to be mistakenly thought of as English. 'My appointment is at midday, but I'm a bit early because the old man wanted to get back to go horse riding.'

It would be quite amazing if her frail 80-year-old husband did go horse riding, but he didn't; Irish Jenny was just a compulsive liar. She had also once told me that she was in constant talks with the government over the possibility of bombing Russia.

'Blast that Putin to bits, I keep telling the Prime Minister!' She had been in the military when she was younger but I somehow doubted that the now 80-year-old Irish woman was advising the government on foreign policy. Although, perhaps the world would be a better place if all foreign policy was dictated by elderly women with chronic IBS. We'd all be dead in no time.

I signed her in for her appointment while she did what most old people did and read off a long list of ailments, aches, pains and medication that she was currently on.

'And now I've got to have this operation,' she complained. 'And my daughter doesn't even have the manners to come and visit me. I tell her that I won't be around forever, so how about showing up to prove to me that you care.'

'Anyway, listen to me blabbering on. I think I'll pop to the loo before my appointment to check if I'm still on my period,' she announced, tottering off to the toilet.

'If she's still on her period then I'm the Queen of Serbia,' Mary quipped, when Jenny had left.

'Serbia doesn't have a queen,' I corrected her

'Not Serbia, I meant Sheba. I bet the old fool doesn't even have a husband.'

'She does, but I'd put money on her not having a daughter.'

'How much?'

'I'm not gambling with you again, Mary.'

'Spoilsport.'

'Do you know anyone who drives a black Audi?' I asked her.

'I know someone who drives a blue Skoda.'

'Not helpful. There's been a black Audi sat outside my flat late at night with their lights on.'

'What's weird about that?'

'Well, no one gets out and no one gets in... they just sit there.'

'It's probably a massive drug dealer selling crack to be honest - your estate is rough as fuck.' Mary had scarcely finished denigrating my heritage when, suddenly, a young couple came rushing through the hospital doors.

The woman, clearly pregnant, was bleeding between her legs, leaving a trail from where the man had abandoned his car.

'Now, *that's* a period!' Mary laughed.

The man held up the bleeding woman as they stumbled towards the desk. The woman was screaming, but it was difficult to tell whether she was screaming in pain or out of sheer fear that she'd lost her child.

Within minutes, Ursula came rushing in, pushing an empty wheelchair. She quickly spotted the patient in question - she was the one crouched over a pool of blood, screaming blue murder. With a great deal of difficulty on Ursula's part, she managed to get her into the chair; the husband just stood there in shock. He was clearly a bit of a drip - *"just like Oliver"* - and was taking the whole situation terribly. Yes, it was his baby too; but it wasn't his genitals that were pouring with blood as he writhed in pain. Still, it's not hospital policy to shake sense into patients, unfortunately.

That was the thing with Malford Hospital; it was so small that the reception doubled up as the local accident and emergency department. One moment we could be checking in an old lady for her haemorrhoids and the next, we could be helping a bloke who's "accidentally" got a TV remote stuck up his arsehole.

Ursula wheeled the woman away and dashed her off to the maternity ward, while the husband just stared at the pool of blood on the floor, then at me and Mary.

'Should I clean it up?' he quivered, before I pointed down the corridor for him to follow his wife, wondering why the hell he was just standing there like a complete twat.

'Sorry,' he whimpered, before setting off into a sprint down the hallway after his wife and Ursula, who had just squeezed into the temperamental lift.

The hospital reception was silent as Mary and I sat behind our desk, quietly finishing our coffees while the hospital cleaner half-heartedly washed away the smelly blood.

'Well, that was exciting!' Mary laughed, finally breaking the silence and cracking open her box of Quality Street that she had stashed under the desk.

'Great, from one disaster to another,' I muttered as I saw Oliver walk through the hospital doors, holding a bunch of flowers and wearing the mustard jacket that I fucking hated.

'Can I help you, dickhead?' I asked, as he approached the desk. He held out the flowers for me, but I just shook my head.

'Well, I was wondering if we could talk for a minute,' Oliver whispered to me, probably hoping that we could pop out for some pissy tea or wild sex. Whatever he wanted, it was going to be unbearable.

'I'm not going out for another pointless drink with you. Mary, go and make me another coffee - we can talk here,' I ordered, which Mary was more than happy with, as she loved a good excuse to leave the reception desk. Plus, she loved drinking lots of coffee as it made her "buzz her tits off".

Oliver stood in front of the reception desk while I sat, leaning back on my chair, with my arms folded and my attitude at peak level. Oliver started by lying that he wasn't sure what our grounds for divorce were.

'Obviously desertion', said Oliver, which made me chuckle. Either he was joking or being retarded.

'I *think* you having sex with another woman doesn't really come under the umbrella of what desertion means, unless it covers you deserting my cunt for someone else's. That's why I've already put adultery,' I said in a light-hearted but condescending tone.

'You deserted me,' Oliver said.

'You slept with another woman,' I replied more seriously.

'Because you deserted me,' Oliver replied.

'I'm not going to say it again. You slept with Claire before I kicked you out and *that's* why we're getting divorced.'

'Is it?'

Oliver loved painting and going to art galleries and getting things completely wrong a lot of the time. At the beginning of our romance, I had found this cute and endearing, but now I found it tedious and irritating. I had also found his hair in the plughole quite sweet, but now, at the end of our marriage, I found it fucking repulsive.

'How's your mother?' he asked, trying to change the conversation.

'Drunk,' I replied, irritated. 'How's Claire?'

'Pregnant.'

'Of course.' I didn't know what to say. 'Well, are we done now? Because I've got lots to do before I leave early for my date. Mary has set me up on a blind date, we're off to the Chinese buffet for our yearly intake of salt,' I lied nastily, hoping that Oliver would bugger off and never come back. It was true; I was actually going to the Chinese buffet, but it was just with Ursula, and Mary had definitely not arranged it.

SANDRA

After an awkward silence where Oliver tried not to cry, he asked me where I had been for the last few days, as my car hadn't been outside my flat and the lights had always been off.

'Are you checking up on me?!' I yelled angrily.

'No, no, I just went past and noticed that's all!' he squealed, stepping away from the desk, realising he'd pushed me a bit too bloody far.

'My car was in for a service and needed repairs, not that it's any of your sodding business.'

So, the black car that was outside my apartment was Oliver's! Of course it was, but I'd never known him to be flash enough to drive an Audi. 'What car are you driving now?'

'Claire's Toyota Prius, why?' he replied confused. Of *course* he drove her twat mobile.

'Not an Audi?'

'No, I wouldn't be seen dead in an Audi,' Oliver replied, slightly offended. 'Horrible cars driven by horrible drivers.' That's probably the only thing that Oliver and I agreed on, although I also thought that BMW and Range Rover drivers were horrible drivers, but unlike Oliver, I wouldn't call them horrible drivers. I'd call them cunts. But which cunt kept parking outside my flat?

Later that evening, as I eventually rolled myself into my cold, crisp bed, full to the brim with Chinese food and Merlot, there was a sudden knock at the door. Who the fuck was that? It was 11pm for fu... oh, of course, it was obviously going to be Oliver. I got out of bed, still wearing my going-out clothes and sleepily opened the door to find Oliver standing there.

'Go home Oliver,' I said, shutting the door on him.

'Why is there a helium canister in the big bins out the back?' he shouted through the door.

'What the fuck are you doing going through the bins?' I whispered angrily, opening the door and dragging him into the apartment. 'When you lived here you never knew where to put the fucking rubbish, but now you don't live here you've suddenly found the bins and have decided to go through them!' I spat at him.

'You're not trying to kill yourself again are you Sandi?' he said, with tears in his eyes and a very concerned look on his face. 'You know you're my one true love.'

'For fuck's sake! No, I'm not, Oliver – and I'm not trying to kill myself again,' I said, lowering my shoulders and easing the expression on my face, trying my best to seem nonchalant and not totally fucking sick with fear.

'Then what were they for?'

'Ursula's birthday balloons if you must know, which you mustn't because it's none of your fucking business,' I said. 'Now please, get the fuck out of my flat!' I pushed him out and closed the door again.

'I don't believe you; we need to talk about this!' Oliver yelled through the door. Luckily, he only kept knocking for another 20 minutes - either that, or he had continued throughout the entire night, but I had been oblivious to it as I had fallen into a deep, drunken sleep.

The next day, I was busy stuffing my face with toast when I heard a knock at the door.

'I swear if that's you again I'll hit you so fucking-' I said as I walked to the door and opened it. 'Hi,' Detective Inspector Roddy said, as he stood there holding an empty helium canister in his hands. 'Can you tell me why this is in your bin please?'

11

Sandra

I stood there for what seemed like an hour but must've only been a few seconds. Roddy asked me the question again.

'Can you tell me why this is in your bin?' I swallowed the brick-sized lump in my throat and tried to slow down my breathing, which had become very quick due to the pure fucking panic that was rushing through me.

'I have,' I cleared my throat loudly, 'started my own party balloon business. I've been using them to blow up balloons, for parties. I put it in the bin because I don't really know what the proper recycling procedure is.' I stared at him. His arrogant smirk wasn't giving anything away.

'Fine, Susan. We were just worried that you might be trying to kill yourself again.' He let out a small laugh. 'Well, I say that *we* were worried, I mean your husband was worried.'

I decided not to correct him on calling me Susan; it would probably work out better for me if he didn't really know my name.

'Yes, Oliver reported that he'd seen the canister and said that you might be trying to kill yourself again. There's a lot of that going around at the moment and it's my duty as the Detective Constable to-'

'Inspector,' I corrected him, without thinking.

'Inspector, thank you love, it's my duty to ensure the safety of the people. And any friend of Mary's is a friend of mine,' Roddy said, smiling. 'So, if you need a friend to talk to, just call 999 and ask for me.' He winked.

When Roddy left, I shut the door and fell immediately to the floor, sweating hard from every pore on my skin and hyperventilating like a crazy bitch.

'Mother fucking balloon business, what the fuckety fuck fuck?!' I hissed, trying to calm down.

Oh Christ, now I didn't know whether to get rid of the rest of the canisters or continue with what I was doing. At that moment, my burner phone beeped in my pocket - a text from the Mother of Dragons, but this was accompanied by two thunderous knocks on the door behind me. I shoved the phone in my pocket, quickly got up off the floor and opened the door with the fakest smile I could muster.

'Sorry to bother you again, Susan.'

'No problem.' My voice quivered.

'I was just wondering… since you run a balloon business, would you be free to attend my niece's birthday party and give all the kids some balloons? Things like superheroes, dinosaurs, naked women with big tits, if ya know what I mean,' Roddy joked, winking at me again.

'Of course.' I lied through my fake smile, slowly dying inside. 'I'd love to.'

12

Roddy

After calling Oliver to tell him that I'd been round to visit his wife (who was smoking hot may I add) and made sure that she wasn't using the helium to kill herself, I popped over to Ingram Road to do some proper police work. Oliver had told me that her name wasn't Susan - it was Sandra - which was strange, because she hadn't corrected me when I'd called her it.

Sadly, Graham's investigation was going slowly and it was making me annoyed; the quicker it was done, the quicker I could spend my time winning over Mary, after which she would drop her knickers and immediately fuck me. But first I needed to interview the dead farmer's neighbours to find out if they'd seen anything suspicious.

Unfortunately, Graham's neighbours were bloody unhelpful as they hadn't seen anything suspicious the night that he had died, but then again there was a huge bushy shrub in between the two farms, so they told me that they never saw anything of him, suspicious or otherwise.

There was one thing that the closest neighbour had noticed, though. One of Graham's cows had got out of the farm and wandered down the road. The neighbour had watched it walk down the road, up until the point when he couldn't see it anymore. Where did it go after that? The neighbour didn't know; he said he wasn't going to follow his dead neighbour's cow down the road and, to be honest, I could see the bloke's point.

I decided that the neighbours were sodding useless and that running around Malford for a stray cow was a thorough waste of police time, but then Dom suggested that we interview the ex-wife. I told him that that was a great idea - and that I had just been about to say the exact same thing.

'It's funny how you've only worked here for a few months and you're already reading my mind.' I chuckled to myself, before looking up the number for Mrs. Oakley and ordering her to the station immediately.

'I've worked here for five years,' Dom replied, but I wasn't really listening to him.

After some toing and froing, Mrs. Oakley, or "Margaret" as she preferred to be called (after she snapped at me the second time I called her Mrs. Oakley), sat opposite me in the police interview room with Dom watching (and probably scratching his arse) through the double-sided glass.

Margaret was not what I'd imagined she'd be like; I thought that she would probably be a bit old, weird and country bumpkin-ish, on account of having been married to a scruffy farmer who liked pine furniture. But she wasn't - instead, she was modern with a nice haircut, good clothes and what looked like a Gucci bag that wasn't one of those knock-offs. I can see who won out of their divorce.

It was clear to me that this rich bird had no reason to kill Graham, but I still interviewed her as if she was our main suspect, mainly because at the moment she was our only suspect.

After double checking whether or not Margaret wanted a lawyer (because I'd forgotten to ask her at the start), I began the interview.

'So, tell me... where were you the night Graham died?' I asked, leaning forward and clasping my hands on the table, like I'd seen on Line of Duty.

'I was at home waiting for one kid to finish football practice and the other kid to come back from ballet.'

'So, your son was at football and your daughter was at ballet,' I said, scribbling on my new notepad.

'No, my *daughter* was at football and my *son* was at ballet,' Margaret said. A girl who played football? Must be a lesbian. God, it was catching! I wondered if Mary liked playing football? I had never seen her play, so hopefully she wasn't 100% lesbian.

After realising that no one could confirm that she was actually at home on her own that night, Margaret started to well up a little. It was clear to me that she was a very smart woman, what with her well-ironed clothes, glasses and the way she used big words. So, if she *had* killed Graham, she would've given herself a bloody good alibi, other than waiting for her kids to come home from their homosexual sports clubs.

'Wouldn't you agree that if I'd killed Graham, that I would've given myself a convincing alibi?' Margaret croaked, a tear running down her face. Holy shit! It was like everyone could read my mind.

'What was your relationship with Graham like?' I asked, trying not to give into the stupid female waterworks that she was clearly putting on.

'Well we were divorced - his idea - he told me to take the kids and the dog and he didn't like visiting them much, so I guess we didn't really have a relationship anymore. I still loved him though.'

But if it was his idea to get divorced, then why had he written such hateful words in the suicide note? He had written that it was Margaret who'd left and taken everything with her - even the dog apparently. But then, she didn't have any dog hair on her clothes so I wondered what she had done with it; maybe she'd shot it? Country people did stuff like that all the time.

'Let's cut the crap Marg,' I said forcefully, leaning back into my chair and crossing my arms. 'You left him, you hated him, you wanted him dead.' Margaret smiled and raised one eyebrow as she herself leaned back into her chair and crossed her arms, mirroring me. Silence lingered for a few seconds as Margaret, or Marg as I had aggressively called her, looked me up and down, trying to work something out in her mind.

'I left him because he was fat, smelly and always had a hand up a cow's arse. He never had time to help the kids with their homework, never had time to be affectionate to me and was too interested in his animals to realise that his family was drifting away from him. That's why I left.'

I opened my mouth to say something witty and clever, but nothing came so I closed it again.

'Did you not know he was a farmer before you got married?' I asked her, confused. Everyone knew that farmers put their arms up cows' backsides, so this really shouldn't have been news to her. Margaret told me that she knew he was a farmer, obviously, but when his mother had died, he'd changed into a grumpy, smelly bore so she left with his kids, most of his money and his dog - but she left the pine.

'You're a horrible woman,' I said without thinking. 'You left a depressed man because he was smelly.'

'He wasn't depressed when I left him and I'm not particularly bothered that he's dead. All I will say is that I was surprised to hear that he had killed himself, I wouldn't've thought he'd have had the balls to do it.' From the smile on her face, I could tell that she was actually rather thrilled that he was dead; I wondered whether his will had anything to do with it.

After another few questions about Margaret's morals and knowledge (or lack of knowledge) about Graham's mental health, I told her that she could go. But as she walked out of the interview room, I told her not to leave the country. She might not be my killer, but she had definitely confirmed the fact that Graham had had help. Perhaps she knew something else that she wasn't telling me.

13

Sandra

'Listen here pal, if you don't sit down and wait your turn, I'm going to call security!' Mary snapped at the man who was screaming at us in front of the reception desk.

'It's an ingrown toenail; I just know it!' The man shrieked. 'Do you know how many people die each year because of an ingrown nail?!'

Did he know how many patients died every year by having their faces smashed onto the Malford hospital reception desk by an angry Scottish lesbian?

'If you don't sit down, you'll soon be wishing that it *was* just your ingrown nail that's hurting.'

'Is that a threat?'

'Absolutely, pal.'

'I'm calling the police!' the man cried, taking his mobile out of his pocket.

'So, you really don't want to be seen by a doctor then? Aye, well no worries.' Mary sat back and crossed her arms.

'What do you mean, I don't want to be seen by a doctor? Of course I want to be seen by a doctor!'

'Then I suggest you put your mobile away, sit down and wait your turn,' Mary said slowly, like she was talking to a stupid child.

After an awkward stare off between the two of them, the man put his phone away and sat back down in the waiting area, while Mary went on the computer and moved his name from the top of the queue to the bottom.

'Sometimes I think I get too much job satisfaction,' she said, taking a drink of her coffee.

'Sometimes I wonder whether you're actually going to assault any of the patients,' I replied.

'Sandra how could you say that?! I might come across as aggressive, but I'm a gentle butterfly.'

'With a Glaswegian tongue.'

'Exactly, I would never actually *hurt* a patient, I just want them all to get better.'

'So they can get out of the hell out of the hospital?'

'Exactly.'

Since Roddy had paid me a visit, I had had an unsettling feeling in my stomach. Either I was going to have an episode of the shits or the local inspector had unnerved me. It normally took a lot to unnerve me, but the prospect of the police finding out about my little suicide service and throwing me in prison filled me with dread.

I needed to make a plan to ensure that I never got caught, and then I needed a back-up plan for when I did get caught. So, the plan I had so far was:

- Only help people to kill themselves if they're depressed or mentally ill; no terminally ill people - I'm not Dignitas on wheels.
- If there's any risk of being caught, get the hell out.
- Only help people who I have zero emotions for. This obviously applies to nearly everyone in Malford.
- Set the scene before leaving; pill bottles (stolen from work), empty alcohol bottles (my recycle bin was constantly overflowing with them) and make sure that it was obvious that the person killed themselves, so that no investigation or post mortem bollocks was carried out.

SANDRA

'Excuse me, I need some help here!' a man cried out, rushing into the hospital, holding up what seemed to be an unconscious woman.

'Here we fucking go,' I muttered, annoyed that my train of suicidal thought had been disturbed.

'I found her in the bath!' the man blurted out, as he plonked the woman over the desk.

'Well, that would explain why she's soaking wet,' Mary said, smiling.

'I think she's tried to kill herself! I don't know if she's taken anything or if she's breathing... please, help her!'

'Let's see if she's still breathing first,' Mary said, eagerly leaning over the counter and putting her ear over the wet woman's mouth. The woman opened her eyes slightly and looked straight at me. 'Yep, she's breathing. Just.'

'We have a semi-unconscious wet woman who needs assistance ASAP,' I told the on-call emergency doctor down the telephone, while the woman continued to stare at me.

'And a man with an ingrown toe!' cried the annoying prick from the waiting area.

'It's your nail that's ingrown, not your toe!' I yelled back at him, '...you fucking *idiot*,' I whispered to myself.

It turned out that the wet woman, who had been rushed in by her friend, had tried to kill herself in the bath. She'd tried to fall asleep lying on her front in a nice hot bubble bath, but what she had forgotten to do first of all, was render herself unconscious.

If I was her, for a start I wouldn't try to fucking drown myself, because that's a horrible way to go; but if I *did* want to drown myself, I'd take a box of codeine, mix it with some Smirnoff and then take a bath. Not that I'd be so stupid as to try and drown myself.

After a long, hard day of checking people into their appointments, dealing with suicidal patients and a bloke with a disgusting toenail, I just wanted to go to my local corner shop, get a bottle of wine or 12 and go home to get drunk.

'What the fuck do you mean I'm banned from buying alcohol?' I yelled a little too loudly at the poor shop assistant, who had shown me a picture of myself with "Don't sell this woman alcohol" written underneath it in my mother's handwriting.

'Has she handed these to every shop?' I asked the timid shop assistant, who nodded fearfully. 'Fuck's sake! Fine, I'll just take 20 Marlboro Reds then please.' The shop assistant shook his head slowly and turned the poster over, to reveal another piece of penmanship from my mother: "And don't let her buy any fags either." My mother really had been busy during her little stay.

After deciding that I couldn't be bothered to drive to the off licenses outside Malford, I thought it might be safe to just go to The Spread Eagle pub and have a few there, before buying some bottles to take home. There's no way that my mother would've given the pubs the poster because she knew that I hated going to pubs - they were far too social and far too expensive. I liked to consume cheap alcohol in the comfort of my own isolated flat.

The Spread Eagle, unbeknownst to me, held its weekly quiz night on Tuesday nights. What was also unknown to me, was that Scottish Mary regularly attended said quiz and immediately spotted me as I opened the pub door. She might have mentioned it to me before to be fair, but most of what she said went straight over my head.

'Look who it is!' Scottish Mary yelled across the pub, as I stood there, still holding the door open and desperately trying to think of an escape. Could I make my excuses and leave? What excuse could I give? That I'd accidentally walked into the pub instead of my flat? No, after the whole suicide bollocks, they'd lock me in a mental hospital at even the tiniest hint of me being insane.

'Hi,' I said, through the biggest smile I could muster. For fuck's sake, I just wanted to get wasted on my own and maybe look on the internet for people with suicidal tendencies. I didn't want to spend the evening with Mary, lovely as she is.

'Is that the girl who committed suicide?' some people in the pub started whispering loudly to each other as I walked up to the bar.

'I heard she hung herself and the rope broke,' one idiot said to another. 'I don't know how the rope broke; she's not *that* fat.'

'Cup of cyanide, please,' I said to the barman, before correcting myself and ordering a wine.

'Well, I heard she slit her wrists but didn't do it deep enough,' another idiot said to his girlfriend.

'And I heard you like cock up your bum but your arsehole is looser than a wizard's sleeve so you can't actually feel it,' I replied, like the nice, polite lady my mother had brought me up to be.

The man blushed bright red and slowly turned away from me to face his girlfriend, who was trying not to laugh. And with that, no one mentioned my suicide attempt again; or at least, not until they all went to work the next day and told everyone about who they had seen in the pub last night.

The Spread Eagle had the Malford Herald newspaper on the bar instead of The Sun; it was a classier establishment than the other shitholes in the town.

"Was Sad Old Farmer Brutally Murdered?" the headline read, with all the tact and sensitivity you'd expect from a local newspaper who really needed to up their circulation. A story about a suspected murder was bloody exciting and it would surely get at least ten more people buying the paper that week. But I'd like to clear something up right now. A) It wasn't a murder, it was an assisted suicide and b) there was nothing brutal about it.

'Who gives a shite?' Mary laughed, folding the paper and throwing it towards the other end of the table. 'Pff... that's nothing; people kill themselves every other week in Glasgow.'

'That's because they live in Glasgow,' I retorted, as I leaned across the table to pick up the newspaper.

'Normally I'd bite your head off for saying shite like that, Sandra, but you've got a bloody point, Glasgow's a dump,' Mary said, finishing off the first of her four pints of Carling that were sat on the table in front of her.

The article described how Graham was an honest, hardworking farmer who was loved by everyone. Even his ex-wife said that Graham had always had her heart, which was nice because she'd left him sod all else.

'He'll be sorely missed in the community,' I read aloud, in disbelief. The only community he'll be sorely missed from is the Graham Oakley farm community that was now exclusively made up of cows and sheep. 'Everyone's a fucking martyr when they're dead, aren't they?' I huffed.

'*Och*, that boils my piss,' Mary said.

'It's like everyone loves someone when they're dead, but when they were alive everyone thought they were a cunt.'

When my dad died everyone had said what a good man he was, but he *was* a good man, they weren't just saying that. Yes, he'd killed people, but it was governed by the American state, so it wasn't murder, it was foreign policy. My American father had come to England after the Vietnam war, met my mum in a Malford butcher's shop and never returned to the USA. He was so traumatised by what he'd seen in the war that when it was over, he wanted to go somewhere boring, plain and ordinarily tedious. Welcome to Malford.

Apparently, I didn't have a choice but to join Mary's quiz team. I didn't mind too much as it meant that we wouldn't have to talk if we were busy answering questions. I just hoped that the quiz was going to be full of easy questions rather than difficult shit that I a) didn't know anything about and b) didn't really care about.

After Mary had told me to stop being such a miserable cow, I went to order another large *pinot grigio* from the bar. When I returned to the table, Mary happily instructed me as to the quiz rules, like a drill sergeant who didn't want any wimpy soldiers holding her back.

No Googling - that was rule number one. Other rules included picking a team captain (that was always Scottish Mary) and choosing a team name that wasn't sweary or inappropriate.

'Shall we call ourselves the Suicide Squad?' one of the women in the team said, which was met with daggers from everyone else. Silly bitch. 'Or perhaps the usual "Let's get quizzical" might be better?' the woman mumbled, raising her glass to her lips and hiding behind it.

Round one was the news round. It covered a large variety of topical news stories from the past week. Mary rubbed her hands together excitedly and smiled a crazy smile that made me wish I was either somewhere else or dead; either would suffice.

There were three other people at the table and everyone finally agreed on a team name: "You're a quizzard, Harry." A fun name - according to Mary, but there was nothing fun about this team, especially as they all had matching quiz t-shirts on with their team's emblem and surname on the back.

I knew that I was going to be rubbish at the first round, especially as I hadn't read the paper properly since I'd been in it (and a few minutes ago, when I'd read about what a great guy Graham was). Also, I didn't know sod all about what had happened in the past week, apart from the fact that I'd performed an assisted suicide and was running out of bin liners. As she sucked her front teeth and raised her eyebrows, Mary made it very clear that she was expecting big things from me.

Round two was the politics round and round three was the television round.

'Round Four, the flower round.'

'Great, my favourite topic,' I muttered under her breath. I'd drunk four large glasses of wine and had answered perhaps one question. I had contributed enough to fuck the fuck off home, 'Mary, I'm gonna go,' I whispered to her, but Mary shushed me loudly like my mum used to when she was on the phone and I was breathing too loudly.

'Which bulb was once used as currency and was even more valuable than gold?' the quiz master asked theatrically.

Mary and the other serious quizzers at the table gossiped wildly, shrugging their shoulders and looking around to see if the other tables were writing anything down. I was busy awkwardly putting my jacket on while still sat down when I paused.

'I think it's tulips,' I whispered, but clearly not quietly enough, because Mary shushed me aggressively again.

'Tulips, are you sure? Could it not be roses, lilies, pansies, daffodils, lily of the valley or hydrangeas?' she asked manically. If I got this wrong, I would never, ever, be invited to take part in her favourite weekly pub quiz again. God, I hoped I was wrong.

'No, I'm pretty sure the Dutch used them as currency,' I said, Oliver and I had been to Amsterdam a few years previously for him to look at art and smoke weed, and I remembered that there were a lot of tulips around. So many, in fact, that I vaguely remembered Googling why they were so popular. Mary jotted down tulips onto the quiz sheet then threw the pen down and leaned back, trying to see whether I was telling the truth or not. Was she pleased with my answer or pissed off with it? Either way, I wouldn't hear the end of it.

Luckily the answer was right, and Mary congratulated me by slapping me very hard on the arm. I didn't know if such violent celebratory smacks on the arm were a lesbian thing, a Scottish thing or just a Mary thing? I suspected it was just a Mary thing and thought it best to avoid all celebratory smacks in future.

As Mary shook her fists in the air, happy that her team (but mainly her) had won The Spread Eagle's weekly pub quiz yet again, I noticed that behind her was a man who seemed to be staring at her oddly.

'Well done, lovey!' Mary yelled at me, shaking my arms in celebration and handing the little crappy trophy to me. The cup of the trophy was so small that it wouldn't even double up as an ashtray. 'Oi dickheads, look who won again!' she laughed across the table to the other pub quiz teams, who all groaned and rolled their eyes as they screwed up their quiz sheets.

'Who's that?' I whispered discreetly to Mary, as she sat down after gloating to every other team in the pub. Mary did a huge 180-degree turn in her chair to see who I was talking about, without an ounce of discretion.

'Oh, that's Benjamin the detective inspector. Ugly bastard, fancies the pants off me,' she laughed, giving him a little wave which he very happily returned.

I looked at him. Holy fuck! Was that the local inspector who had come to my flat? He looked a lot different in his football shirt while staring at Mary with what can only be described as teenage lust. After gathering up the courage, he stood up, wiped his shirt clean of crisps and approached our table.

'Detective Inspector Benjamin Roddy, good friend of dear Mary here,' he said, holding his hand out to me as I was finishing my last tiny drop of wine, ready to get the fuck home. 'Oh, it's *you*.'

'Yes it is. Nice to see you. Mary, I'm going to go now,' I said as normally as possible, trying not to collapse, puke and shit myself all at the same time.

'Don't go because of this twat! He's not scared you off has he? He's not scary, he just sits on his fat arse all day!' Mary laughed.

'I most certainly do not! In fact, I'm currently investigating a murder,' Roddy said in a bizarre Scottish accent, trying to mimic Taggart. 'Oh wait, no, I'm not meant to say anything about that. Ignore me... not a murder, just a suicide.' He smiled, blushing a beautiful bright shade of red that matched the ketchup on his shirt.

'A murder, you say?' Mary said in her thickest Scottish accent, taking the piss out of everyone who had ever asked her to say that "there's been a murder". She turned her head up to look at Roddy, who was still brighter than a London bus. He let out a big breath and tried to calm himself.

'Yes, a murder. Well, it's actually more of a suicide, but nevertheless, someone in Malford has died,' he said, quietly leaning into the two of us so no one else could hear, even though it was spread across the front of the newspaper.

'Someone else in Malford has died?!' someone from across the other side of the bar shouted, making everyone in the pub gasp like they were in some shit 70s comedy sketch.

'Murdered!' Scottish Mary yelled loudly, making everyone gasp again. I was now redder than Roddy, sat frozen in my seat, gripping tightly onto my empty glass of wine. Detective? Fuck. A suicide that could be a murder? Double fuck. An empty glass of wine?! Well, you get the gist.

14

Sandra

Sat in the circle of love, acceptance and all that bollocks were me and 11 other crazy men and women suffering from mental illness. I didn't believe that I had any sort of mental problems, especially not like the ones that the people around me had, but it was either this or be forced to move in with my mother, so I happily chose the former.

The moderator sat down on her giant bean bag that only she was allowed to sit on and slapped her hands on her thighs, signalling to everyone that it was time to begin. On the floor next to her was a fluffy teddy bear; only those with "Mr. Schnitzel" were allowed to speak. Because obviously we adults, most of whom were at least 30 years old, couldn't be trusted to let each other speak without interrupting.

'Hello everyone, my name is Mitzi and I've got a mental health problem,' the moderator said, without holding Mr. Schnitzel, which was a complete violation of the house rules. I'd also found out from work that Mitzi had a huge LSD problem, but she had failed to mention that at the group.

'Hello, Mitzi,' we all replied together. Again, no one was holding Mr. Schnitzel. The house rules were certainly not being upheld - what a disaster. However, with Mitzi's very temperamental nature and horrendous drug problem, the fact that people spoke without holding the teddy was the least of the group's worries. Mitzi had the same hair as me and was of a similar build as well, but she wore tie-dye clothes that she made herself and only ever walked around barefooted; Oliver would cum immediately in his pants if he saw her.

'This is a safe space for everyone to express their issues without feeling judged or embarrassed. I see some old faces here today and I see a new face next to Sandra. Hello there, take Mr. Schnitzel and introduce yourself,' she said to the lady, as she picked up the teddy from the floor and passed it round to her.

To be honest, I hadn't paid much attention to the woman sitting next to me, because what I liked to do at these meetings was say fuck all and try my best to fall asleep with my eyes open, before buggering off home. I definitely hadn't noticed her when she had first taken her seat, but now that I turned to look at her as she introduced herself, I instantly recognised her.

'Hello,' the woman said through a flood of tears that started as soon as she took the teddy. 'My name is Leanne,' she continued through her heavy sobbing. 'Last week, I tried to kill myself,' more loud sobs escaped from her mouth, 'in the bath!' Even more loud sobs filled the room.

She went on to explain, in between crying, that she had been depressed since she was 16, when her best friend told her to never contact her again. Apparently, Leanne had been in unrequited love with said friend, but he had had enough of her. Cut to twenty years later and Leanne seemed to be the same miserable, unhappy sap that she had been when she was a teenager. Of course, I'm just assuming that from what she was saying - she could be the right soul of the party.

'I've got no one apart from maybe one friend, but even he doesn't like me,' Leanne ended. Yep, a total sap. Everyone stared at her with blank faces, apart from Mitzi, who was in floods of tears. She was often in a state, being the most mentally unstable person in the group.

'I'll go next!' shouted Bailey, the group alcoholic, who had only joined the group because he was banned from Alcoholics Anonymous

SANDRA

for being drunk. 'I've had a really shit week. Got arrested for being drunk and disorderly when robbing the bank on Monday. The pigs gave me this black eye,' he said, pointing to his huge purple bruised eye.

'Excuse me Mr. Bailey, but you do not have Mr. Schnitzel! Bath lady, give the man the teddy please!' Mitzi snapped at Leanne, who was too busy crying. She handed the teddy to me and I passed it around the circle. Leanne looked at me for a few seconds longer than was socially acceptable; she'd recognised me, but I just smiled and turned my face away.

'Where was this bank you robbed, Bailey?' Mitzi asked, with a big smile on her face, happy that the group's rule of "no talking unless holding Mr. Schnitzel" was being upheld.

'I went down to Cornwall for a few days - heard they got good scrumpy didn't I?' Bailey then spent the next 20 minutes repeating how his alcohol problem had started as a baby thanks to his alcoholic parents, who never had any milk but had always had Baileys in the house - hence his name.

When the meeting ended, I got up and was walking quickly to the door when someone tapped me on the shoulder. It was Leanne. I turned around, trying to act normally, not like I was rushing out of the door to avoid her.

'You work at the hospital,' Leanne said.

'I do,' I replied, while trying to see out of the corner of my eyes whether anyone was watching. They weren't; everyone was too busy signing up for Mitzi's new anxiety retreat in Dartford to pay attention to Leanne and me, 'but I'm just the receptionist.'

Leanne, who had dried her tears slightly by this point, asked me if I would talk to her for a moment. Maybe in my car instead of in front of everyone? Leanne wanted to tell me what had happened in the bath and then kept asking me what she needed to do to kill herself properly. I felt like telling her not to be so fucking stupid as to try and drown herself, but instead, I began to tell her all the different ways she could do it properly.

'You could get me pills,' she interrupted manically, smiling wildly.

'I can't get you pills, I'm just the receptionist. Unless it's paracetamol you want.'

'Will that kill me?'

'No,' I replied. The memory of puking up in the back of an ambulance came flooding back.

'Aren't you the woman from the paper?' she asked.

'Depends which paper you're talking about.'

'The Malford Herald.'

'Then it depends which article you mean.'

'The one about the woman who tried to kill herself after her dad did the same thing,' she said cautiously, in case she had got it wrong.

'Yup, that's me.'

'Oh, then don't worry, I don't want you to help me,' she said, sitting up straight and looking out at the road ahead.

'Why not?' I asked, a tiny bit offended.

'I don't mean to offend you, but if you failed at it then you won't be able to help me, will you?'

'That's where you're wrong.' I sighed, after deciding that I would help her. The only qualm I had about it was because it was only a few days away from my appointment with the Mother of Dragons and even Hitler hadn't moved this quickly in the beginning. 'I know a guaranteed, painless and easy way.'

I paused for a second. Was I going to do this? Adrenaline rushed through my veins and it felt fucking amazing, but a small pang of guilt also wavered in my stomach. 'I can help you.' And that was when I gave a similar spiel that I had given to Graham about what the procedure was, and how I would perform it whilst minimising all risks of getting caught - not that Leanne seemed to care much as she was too busy crying; with happiness, I presumed.

Two hours later, I left her place and made my way home feeling great. What an exciting evening it had turned out to be! However, when I got home, I noticed the black Audi sat outside. This time, no one was in the driver's seat, so I went to have a nose around the car but there was nothing inside. I dragged my suitcase quickly through my apartment block's main doorway and up the two flights of stairs to my flat, where I stood, exhausted outside my front door, trying to find my keys. But as I put the key in the lock, my door opened; someone was *inside* my flat.

'Where have you been?' Oliver demanded, standing there, holding the door open from the inside. I stood there in shock with the blood rushing to my face. What the fuck was this dickhead doing in my flat? I quickly returned back to my normal "couldn't give a shit" self as I barged past him and into my apartment.

'I went on a date actually, a really successful one,' I lied, as I pulled my suitcase into the flat and set it down behind the sofa before returning to the front door and folding my arms, looking at Oliver expectantly.

'We're not divorced yet, Sandi,' Oliver said, shaking the divorce papers in his hand, 'I'm not happy with you going out on dates; you're not fully recovered from your suicide attempt yet. And why did you take a suitcase with you?' he asked, confused at the mysterious object.

'The suitcase is full of all my anal sex toys and I don't care if you're not happy, now fuck off back to your Audi,' I replied flippantly. Oliver opened his mouth but closed it again abruptly. His eyes filled up with tears, hurt from my harsh-but-true words.

'I don't have an Audi, how dare you! You haven't always been this much of a bitch!'

'Yes I have, I just got fed up with hiding it. What do you want Oliver? I've had a long day and- how did you get into my apartment?'

'I got a spare key cut from the one you keep under the mat,' Oliver replied.

'Well, I'll have it back now.'

'Oh, will you?'

'Stop pissing me about and get out or I'm going to call the police,' I threatened, backing him towards the open front door. My fear of being caught finishing someone off, mixed with Oliver's usual irritating-self was a bad combination, and unless Oliver wanted to be taken out on a stretcher, he had better get the fuck out. These suicides were really fuelling my internal fire that I thought had gone out a while ago. Even Oliver couldn't ruin this buzz.

15

Sandra

Unlike the actual Mother of Dragons, my one lived in a 2-bed terrace with a mattress on the front lawn and sod all parking out the front; not that I was going to park directly outside the house, obviously. I parked around the back and gave him a call. I hadn't spoken to him yet as we had only texted, so it was strange when he answered. He sounded exactly like I thought he would; gruff, with tones of low self-esteem.

'Hi, just checking you're still in and ready?' I asked, being careful with my choice of words in case he had me on loudspeaker, waiting in a circle of police officers. In the event that he had told the police, I had brought a handful of empty character balloons as a cover-up. It was sort of lucky that Oliver/Roddy had forced me to make up this bollocks balloon business, because now I had a good cover.

'Yes,' he answered dully.

'Great, can you come out the back of your house?' I asked.

'Come round the front,' he replied flatly, though by the sounds of his sluggish voice, he wouldn't have cared if I'd come in through the ceiling.

'No.' I replied.

'Why?' he asked.

'Because that would be really sodding suspicious wouldn't it?' I snapped back, a little shorter of patience than usual. I wasn't as nervous as I'd been with Graham, but I was still apprehensive, having not met the bloke before.

The phone went dead and I thought I'd fucked up my chances, when suddenly I heard a loud, stiff door opening at the back of the terraced houses. I saw a man step out and raise his hand half-heartedly in the air for me to see. I took a deep breath and walked towards the house, pulling my suitcase along behind me.

The Mother of Dragons, or Clive, as it said on his unopened post in the kitchen, had grey-brown hair, a large stomach and the look of someone who had worked in hospitality for 30 years. His house was full of rubbish, dirt and rodent droppings, most likely from the five guinea pigs that were currently running around on the sofa next to their open cage. Clive told me that he had wanted to commit suicide for a while, but his depression had stopped him from finding the motivation to do it.

'I know what you mean Clive–'

'It's Khaleesi.' he corrected me.

'Is it? Right, well, I know what you mean. The depression keeps you trapped inside your own head so that you can do nothing but eat, drink and smoke.'

'And breed guinea pigs,' he added.

'Right. And breed guinea pigs.'

'How are you going to put me out of my misery?' he asked, looking up at me pathetically.

Once I'd told him exactly how we were going to do it, to which he had no reaction at all, I told him to go upstairs, put on his ghost outfit and climb into bed. But Clive had other ideas. He told me that he wanted to die on his favourite sofa, surrounded by his guinea pig children, in the clothes he was already wearing.

'Very well, if you're sure. I'll get you all set up,' I said, as I laid my suitcase down and started taking out my equipment piece by piece.

Clive looked at it all, but his nonchalant face never changed expression. Even when I put the silicon gel on his face and placed the mask over his nose and mouth, he had the same, bored, hopeless look.

'Are you ready Clive?' I asked him, as I perched on the chair opposite him with the helium canister between my legs.

'My name is Khaleesi,' he said through the mask, as he picked up two of the guinea pigs and put them on his lap.

'No it's not. Are you ready?'

'Hash Anna,' he whispered.

'What?' I guessed that "hash anna" was some Dothraki bullshit for "yes", but I needed to hear it in English - thank you very much.

'Yes, do it,' he groaned.

Very slowly, I turned the nozzle and let the helium rush up the tube, around the bends, into the mask, and into Khaleesi's mouth, before it started swimming down into his lungs and finally arriving in his bloodstream.

He said nothing as he sat stroking his guinea pigs, his hand movements eventually getting slower and slower. Unlike Graham, he didn't take very long to fall into unconsciousness. His hand stopped and his head collapsed onto his chest. Seeing this opportunity for freedom, the guinea pigs made their little squeaking noises and began running around Clive's lap, before starting to chew through his joggers.

I sat, patiently waiting on the chair while nosing at the picture frames around the room. The frames were tatty and old, and the pictures looked like they were the ones that had come with the frames.

A loud, bizarre fart followed by some large air bubbles escaped from Clive's groin area, that made even the guinea pigs freeze with fear. A smell of foul death reached my nostrils and I ran into the kitchen to dry heave into the sink. Jesus fucking Christ, I didn't know that living people could make a smell that rotten.

I wondered whether guinea pigs, like dogs, had a heightened sense of smell, because if they did then they would be dying from the horrendous stench any minute now. Even though I hated most living things, including guinea pigs, they were actually quite cute with their different colours and scruffy hair. It's a shame that Clive hadn't bothered to sort out any permanent accommodation for his furry friends before our appointment. Selfish prick.

Once he was dead, I cleaned away my tools, wiped the gel off his face and triple checked his pulse. Maybe in future I should bring a stethoscope with me, just to make sure that my special patients were definitely dead. I wouldn't want any surprise visits from someone I'd failed to kill.

Taking the empty bottles of tablets and alcohol out of my suitcase I placed them creatively around him on the sofa. The brown guinea pig immediately approached the vodka bottle and stared to nibble at the lid.

Walking out of the living room and into the kitchen towards the back door, I noticed a stash of unopened wine bottles lined up next to the cooker. Why hadn't I noticed them on the way in? Could I take them with me? It took me a couple of minutes to decide that even though I loved wine, I had morals; morals that told me that it was okay to kill a depressed smelly man with his rodent children by his side, but it was not okay to then steal his alcohol stash on the way out.

I quietly opened the rather stiff backdoor and lifted my suitcase out onto the patio. I was carefully closing the door behind me when I stopped. Come on Sandra, of course you can't leave without stealing them... was it even technically still stealing if the owner was dead? I decided that it wasn't.

The guinea pigs that I had "stolen" and squeezed into their cages, squeaked and pooped constantly. I had to be going soft or some bullshit, because the old me would've stolen the alcohol and left the animals. Maybe I just didn't want the little creatures to die from the rotten stench that had escaped their owner's arsehole at the time of death, either that or I just liked the idea of having another living thing in my flat.

Clive had been a bit different to Graham; there had been some sadness with Graham because he had told me all about his life and his

SANDRA

divorce. But Clive hadn't wanted to tell me fuck all, apart from that he had depression, was bipolar and wanted to be referred to as some character from Game of Thrones. It was his prerogative of course, and perhaps the fact that he didn't tell me much had made it easier to carry out the task and feel almost completely guilt free.

On the way back home, my phone rang. It was Ursula.

'Darling, how are you? Where are you?' she asked, which made me suddenly feel sick with worry, because Ursula never asked me where I was unless I was late for work. Even then, it would usually be Mary who called.

'I'm just coming back from a job,' I said, without my brain giving a single fucking thought as to what I was saying.

'A job? What are you talking about, sweetie?'

'I've started a new business... a balloon business... you know, blowing up balloons for parties. We can't all be on the head of midwifery wage.' I stumbled over my words. Ursula fell silent for a while, before deciding that I was obviously talking absolute bollocks.

'Oh Sandi, I thought you'd cut down on your drinking now that your mother's banned you from the off licenses. Anyway, I need your help ASAP, so get over to my house quickly. Get a taxi, I'll pay. I'll just take it out of my head of midwifery wage,' she joked.

I didn't know what the hell she wanted, but I hoped that it was a) going to be fucking quick and b) involved alcohol, because I needed to celebrate another successful suicide. It had gone absolutely swimmingly, no problems whatsoever - unless you count me suddenly becoming a mother of five guinea pigs as being a problem.

My buzz from the success soon fizzled out when I stepped into Ursula's house to find four of my colleagues holding party balloons, cake and happy sodding grins on their faces. It was my birthday and I had forgotten.

'Happy birthday Sandi! Why have you got a cage full of guinea pigs?' Ursula laughed, giving me a hug and handing me a glass full of cold white wine, which I downed pretty bloody quickly.

'Oh, they're for your kids. Do they like guinea pigs?' I said, putting the cage on the counter. I wasn't destined to be anyone's mother, even if it was just to five cute, hairy rodents.

'No, they're allergic to them. Take it easy Sandi,' she replied, looking strangely from my wine glass to the guinea pig cage.

Mary was there, as was the new doctor, Alec, and so was Rosie from paediatrics. Great! I loved social events, especially ones that happened by surprise after I'd just helped kill the Mother of Dragons before immediately becoming the mother of five guinea pigs.

I lied that I hadn't eaten so that I could just tuck into the cake instead of having to talk to anyone, but that only lasted twenty minutes.

'So, Sandra is it? How old are you today?' Alec asked, as he swooned up to me like a sleazier James Bond. I looked at him and wondered why the fuck he was here. I'd never spoken to him and he'd never spoken to me, so I ignored him and instead took my guinea pig cage and walked over to Mary.

'Such a shame about that farmer, did anyone else see that in the news?' Alec asked everyone in the room. Oh fuck off Alec, yes everyone had fucking seen the news but it was over two weeks ago so get over it already.

'Terrible shame,' Ursula said in agreement. Alec walked over to her and touched the small of her back with his hand. She smiled and winked at him before quickly walking away to chat to Rosie, but it was clear from the wink and the redness of Ursula's cheeks that something was going on between them. Ursula was happy, married and bloody rich, so why she would even consider doing anything to jeopardise that was beyond me.

'I couldn't give a shite about that farmer, but I was told by the fat detective that it's now a murder inquiry,' Mary boasted, as she took a large swig of her beer. Ursula had offered Mary a glass for the cans of Stella that she'd brought round, but Mary had deliberately turned it down. They just loved to piss each other off like that. Mary liked to call Ursula a tampon because she was so stuck up. Ursula was too posh to call Mary such names, but she hated her equally.

'A murder inquiry?!' Rosie gasped.

'Blimey, that's terrible news.' Ursula said, covering her mouth in shock. I didn't know why everyone was so shocked about it being a murder inquiry. People get murdered all the time, and anyway, it wasn't bloody murder. I guess that Ursula was upset because she had kids and a murderer on the loose could pose a threat to their existence.

Everyone went on and on about how they had seen the farmer at the hospital before and how devastating it was that he was dead. Ha! They wouldn't be saying that if they'd heard him on the bridge. I was busy chomping on some more cake while downing some serious glasses of wine, as I watched Alec constantly touching Ursula when he thought no one was looking.

'Sorry, but is this my fucking surprise birthday party or some sort of dead farmers appreciation society?' I blurted out drunkenly, after finishing my sixth glass of wine in just 45 minutes. Alec and Rosie grinned at each other to stop themselves from laughing at my outburst, Mary just raised her eyebrow and cracked opened another can of beer and Ursula shook her head and gave me a big hug.

'I'm sorry darling, why don't you make a speech?' she asked kindly. She always said things kindly, being a mother and all that.

'Because I'm not a best man at a wedding,' I mumbled, staggering over to get another bottle of wine out of the fridge.

'How about you make a quick speech and then we'll all toast your birthday… with some of the children's squash.'

'I'm not a, *hiccup*, child,' I said to Ursula, looking at my new pet guinea pigs.

'Of course not sweetie, a child wouldn't have this sort of drinking problem.'

For some reason, Ursula ushered me towards the sink to make my birthday speech.

'Thanks Mary and Rosie for coming and ta for the party Ursula. And Alec, I'm not really sure what you're doing here.' I pointed at him drunkenly. 'If I'm honest, I didn't think I'd get to this birthday because I thought that I would've been digested a hundred times over by worms by now. Anyway, happy birthday me!' I said, when suddenly a huge avalanche of alcohol and cake rose up out of my throat and into my mouth. I spun round and threw up in the sink. 'So that's why you moved me to the sink,' I mumbled to Ursula as I came up for air. Maybe Clive's suicide had affected me more than I'd thought.

16

Roddy

'Another suicide, Roddy,' said Dom, the only other police officer in Malford Police Station.

'Probably nothing interesting,' I said, shrugging it off while continuing to scroll through my phone and eat my lunch.

'Leanne Lewis.'

'The psycho bird who tried to drown herself? Is it definitely suicide?'

'Well, that's what the person who found her said.'

'And who was the person who found her dead?'

'I don't know, boss.'

'What *do* you know Dom?'

'Not a lot boss.'

'Right, well get your coat on and meet me in the Beemer,' I ordered, as I threw the radio on the desk, frantically put my shoes back on and shoved the remaining chips into my gob.

Having been to my first post-mortem and found some key evidence on Graham's computer, I was starting to feel more confident and professional. Obviously, I hadn't *completely* forgotten about the slightly unfortunate moment at the pub quiz when I'd announced that Graham's suicide wasn't actually suicide, and also the chewing gum incident at the post-mortem. But now I was feeling bold enough to swing my dick around this new crime scene; today was going to be an excellent day.

We entered the flat, which was covered in baby clothes and toys that still had the labels on to find Leanne and her distraught friend in the bedroom; one was clearly sad and the other was clearly dead.

'Any suicide note?' I asked the friend. She shook her head and looked around the room through her tears.

'Right, we're all going to have to evacuate this flat as it's now a crime scene and anyone of us could contaminate it.' I took a good look at Leanne. She was white as a ghost, which I thought was funny, because she technically *was* a ghost now.

'They'll probably have to pop out her ribcage and take her lungs out to do a toxicology report,' I said, nodding to myself, satisfied that I'd made myself look really intelligent in front of Dom.

'They'll have to do *what?!*' the friend shrieked, before going into another hysterical crying fit.

'This is a crime scene love, you'll have to leave.' The friend walked out in tears and waited in the corridor.

I followed her and made a few phone calls to get forensics to the scene. A few minutes later, Dom walked out with a suicide note in his hand.

'She *did* write a note, Boss.'

'What took you so long to find it?' I said, snatching the note out of Dom's hand. 'To whoever finds my body, I'm so sorry. Leanne.' I read the note aloud and put it in my pocket. A bit of a cold suicide note for a bird; normally they're full of sentimental lovey-dovey stuff.

The three of us stood in silence, waiting in the corridor, but the doors were still wide open so all three of us could still see Leanne's dead body slumped over in the bed.

'I know I'm not the detective inspector here,' Dom began to say.

'Well done, dippy,' I replied.

'But aren't we allowed to be waiting in the flat? Us being the police?' Dom said, and the friend who was still crying nodded in agreement.

'You're right, Dom. You're *not* the detective inspector here, so shut your pie hole.'

'But-'
'No!'
'But, Boss-'
'Dom, who pays your wages?'
'Um, the taxpayer.'
'Yes, well *I'm* a taxpayer so *I* pay your wages and *I'm* telling you to shut the hell up and wait.'

I remained silent, standing with my hands in my pockets and my chin up while waiting for forensics to get there.

'You know you don't have to wait outside Roddy; this is your crime scene,' the forensic guy laughed, when he eventually turned up and entered the flat.

'See, told you we didn't have to wait out here Dom, you plonker,' I said, putting my right foot out and marching back into the flat.

'You aren't needed anymore, but if we find that we do need you, we'll contact you,' I said to the friend, who burst into more tears as she walked down the corridor towards the stairs.

'Did you get her contact details, boss?' Dom asked, closing the flat door behind me as he got out his big ass camera ready to take photos.

'I know that lady, we go to the same swimming pool,' I lied. I didn't go swimming - swimming was for kids and sissies.

'This is Malford, everyone goes to the same swimming pool boss...'

The forensics guy told me that he had found nothing suspicious apart from the fact that, like Graham, there was no clear sign of suicide, even with the suicide note. After the scene had been examined and all necessary things taken into evidence, the big black Femidom coroner was called to take the body away, so I quickly skedaddled before he told anyone about the whole chewing gum incident.

'Hey, forensics guy,' I called out, before the guy got into his car. He walked back over to where Dom and I were standing outside the block of flats. 'What do you think happened here?'

'Well, I'm not the detective here.'

'Neither is he,' Dom muttered to himself.

'It's not similar to the scene back at the farm because this woman was surrounded by empty alcohol and pill bottles and the farmer wasn't.'

'Oh yeah…'

'Also, the whole set up tells me that someone has been watching too many 80s films, because people don't take an overdose, down two bottles of vodka and leave the bottles creatively scattered around the bed like that. So, I'd probably say it was foul play which was then made to look like a suicide. Or-'

'Yes?'

'It could be something really crazy, where a few people have gotten together and come up with a way to kill themselves. One person helps someone kill themselves and then they get someone to keep them kill themselves and so on and so on,' the forensic guy said through a laugh as he lit up a cigarette.

'A bit like dominos?' I asked.

'Yeah, a bit like dominos.' He blew out a cloud of smoke and I coughed in annoyance. 'Just a wacky theory, Rodders,' he said, winking at me.

'Well yes, that's true, it *is* just a theory, although it's exactly the same theory that I had. Hopefully it's something a lot less sinister than that,' I said, hoping that it was actually just something a lot less complicated; less complicated meant less work for me and more time to learn how to woo my sweet Scottish Mary.

'There was a mental health meeting poster on her fridge,' Dom said, while messing about on his camera. The forensic guy and I looked over to Dom, who looked up from his camera, confused at the sudden attention on him.

'Looks like he's more of a detective than you are Rodders,' the forensic guy said jokingly, hitting me hard on the shoulder. I looked at him with disgust.

'Fuck off, Dave.'

'My name's Patrick.'

'Fuck off, Patrick.'

17

Sandra

'So much bloody traffic this morning!' I said to Ursula, as I threw my bag into my locker and slammed the door, but Ursula was too busy staring intently at her phone to answer. 'You alright?' I asked, when she failed to acknowledge that I was in the room.

'Sorry darling,' she said, shaking her head and putting her phone in her pocket. 'Having marriage troubles. The pillock thinks it's alright for him to go on a stag do to Thailand for 10 days without even asking me. Yes, traffic, atrocious darling,' she said, whisking herself out of the staff room.

With ten minutes left before I started my shift and Ursula not being in a very chatty mood for our usual pre-shift gossip, I went to visit the bowel ward and found Irish Jenny sat up in bed, reading a magazine. Being an older woman, Jenny had a calming and cheerful presence that appeased me and made me forget about all the suicide bollocks that had been dominating my life for the past few months.

'I just don't see why my daughter can't visit her mother in the hospital. It's not as if she's got a boyfriend or anything. Don't have any kids, Sandra; they'll take you for all you've got then they'll bugger off in times of need. At least I've got this idiot,' she said, popping a grape into her mouth and looking over at her "stupid lump of a husband", who was sat next to her. Jenny offered me the bag, so I took a small bundle of grapes and smiled pityingly at John.

'Sandra, darling, I need to speak with you,' Ursula said, bursting into the bowel ward with urgency. I stood up quickly and said goodbye to Jenny.

'I'll visit you again after your operation, Jenny.'

'Ok Dear, go and save lives!' she hollered, as I followed Ursula out of the ward; I was going to turn back around and remind Irish Jenny that I was just the receptionist, but I couldn't be bothered.

Ursula pushed her way into the empty staff room and closed the door quickly behind me as I stood, confused, wondering what the emergency was.

'He's going to have an affair,' Ursula blurted out.

'How do you know?'

'I just know,' she replied, bursting into floods of tears. I went over to console her.

'Well, he might no-'

'He's been acting really weird and now this!' Ursula cried.

'He might just be having a mid-life crisis,' I said, gently rubbing my friend's back.

'He's 34! That's not midlife! Unless he dies at 68, but if I'm right about the cheating he'll be long dead before then. There's a *woman* going on this stag do.' Ursula burst into another fit of wailing. Was this a good time to ask her about what was going on between her and the new doctor, Alec? Probably not.

'Listen, I'm guessing there's a lot of guys on this stag do, so he isn't going to do anything with everyone watching. And if he does, then I'll kill him myself. I could do it-' I stopped dead. What the fuck was I saying?

'What are you saying Sandi? Have you just offered to kill my husband?' Ursula laughed, wiping away her tears.

'No, I'm obviously not going to kill him,' I replied. Ursula stared at me with confusion for a few moments.

'Well, I'm sure you're right. I'm sure I'm just being silly and it'll all be fine. Thank you, sweetie.' She hugged me, wiped her tears away and shook her head, bringing herself back to reality. 'You're a good friend. Anyway, how are you doing?' she asked.

'I'm doing ok, but I've still got a terrible pain in my liver-'

'-And your drinking isn't going to help,' Ursula interrupted.

'And my drinking isn't going to help my liver, but it sure as hell helps my mind.' I paused and looked at the floor. I couldn't tell Ursula about my new hobby, could I? 'I've got a new hobby that's keeping me busy,' I said, looking up at Ursula. I could tell my best friend - maybe she'd be fine with it, maybe she'd be really supportive. 'I've started…' On second thoughts, maybe not. '…A balloon business,' I said, confused at the words that were coming out of my mouth. I could've said that I had taken up bricklaying or extreme ironing and it would've been more believable. But if I was going to lie to everyone about what I was doing I would have to be consistent.

'Balloons? So, it wasn't a lie when you said, on your birthday, that you'd been working your other job?' Ursula asked, her eyebrows so far up her face that they almost reached her hairline.

'Yes, balloons,' I nodded.

'Well, that's great, Sandi! Whatever brings you happiness and makes you feel better. I've heard lots of people have turned to the church in times of hardship, but I'm sure balloons are just as good,' she said, looking at me strangely. 'Anyhoo, must go, those babies aren't going to deliver themselves!' she chirped, as she walked out of the staff room as if she hadn't broken down in tears just a few minutes ago.

I briefly looked at the front page of the paper that was on the table as I walked out of the staff room. A picture of Leanne stared back at me. Her suicide had made the news headlines just two days after it had happened; the sad story of a crazy psycho killing herself a mere two weeks after the farmer had done the same, would sell a shit load of papers.

I really needed to chill the hell out with all these lies and suicides; it was becoming a bit too sodding much. When I had seen Graham on the bridge, it was only meant to be a one-off, but now I was killing on the daily, in between being an alcoholic and balloon entrepreneur.

The reception was noticeably devoid of patients and noise, with a very rough looking Mary leaning on both hands to hold her head up. A sweet, old lady came toddling through the doors and up to Mary, who was still a little bit drunk.

'I once had an English lass who liked to dress up, ya know, a bit of sexy role play,' Mary began.

'Please don't tell me anymore,' I told her.

'I dressed up as William Wallace and she was dressed as Edward the first.'

'Excellent, now I will never get that image out of my head.'

'Can you tell me where the maternity ward is dear?' asked the old lady.

'Oh, it's you Doris,' I said, almost happy to recognise the old lady's friendly face. 'You're not expecting, are you?' I asked, pointing towards her belly, at which Doris chuckled a sweet little old lady chuckle.

'Our friend just had another grandchild, so I thought I'd come up and see it.'

'The maternity ward is on the ground floor down that corridor. If you're free after, how about we grab a coffee?' I asked, feeling surprisingly happy with the social interaction. We agreed to meet in the hospital canteen during my lunch break.

'Well, it's a very ugly baby but all babies are ugly, aren't they? Covered in poo with a squished-up face, but you can't say that to the parents though of course. To them he's a beautiful little cherub,' Doris laughed, taking a sip of tea and cutting into a section of her carrot cake.

'When Oliver and I first got married, my mother kept on about when we were going to make her a grandmother and said we were selfish for delaying it. Selfish? For not wanting to shove another human being out of my cu-...lady garden?' I said, censoring myself in between bites of cake.

'I was lucky; my mother knew I wasn't going to have any babies, so she never asked.'

Doris had been a frequent visitor to the hospital and after I'd seen her a few times in reception, I'd decided to strike up a sort of friendship and occasionally visit her in the bowel ward. She was nearly always in the bowel ward, due to her IBS and hernias.

'Last time I was here for that hernia operation, there was a rumour. I don't like to listen to gossip, but-' Doris hinted, smiling shyly at me.

I took a long deep breath before giving my answer. I didn't like to keep sharing the story; maybe I should write a book about it and just hand it out.

'My father hung himself,' I revealed, trying to play it down so Doris wouldn't grill me for all the details.

'Oh dear, me and my big mouth. I'm so sorry love.'

'It's ok. Well, it's not, but it was a year ago now. I found him swinging in the garage, so I decided to take an overdose and kill myself, but unfortunately and bizarrely, I didn't take enough,' I blurted out in one huge breath.

She took my hand over the table and rubbed it kindly, smiling at me, unsure of what to say. We finished our coffee and cake while Doris confided in me about the blood that she had found in her stool. I told her that she needed to have it checked out.

During my time working at the hospital, I had come across a lot of absolute wankers, but sometimes a special patient that I didn't completely despise would come along and a friendship would be made. Doris was one of them.

We walked towards the staff car park together, reminiscing about Doris's medical history and discussing her recent bowel problems.

'Are you sure you don't mind giving me a lift, dear?' Doris asked.

'Of course not. Mary will be absolutely fine. She loves working on her own while suffering from an horrendous hangover,' I said, unlocking the car and opening the passenger door for Doris to get in. 'You need to get that stool looked at, by the way.'

'It's just my IBS. Wow, this is an old car!' Doris giggled, as she settled into the passenger seat, admiring the vintage interior and completely ignoring what I had just said.

'It was my mum's car before she buggered off to Spain.'

I drove to Doris's house and gave her my number in case she ever needed to call me. I also reminded her to get her stool checked out again.

'Take it, just in case you ever need me,' I said, hugging Doris after walking her to her door, where her husband Frank was waiting for her. Frank stood, hunched over, holding the front door open for his wife of 59 years. She walked up to him and kissed him before saying goodbye to me and stepping inside.

'Are you sure you won't come in for a cup of tea?' Frank asked me.

'I've got to get back to work. Mary will make me buy her lunch for a week again if I'm any later. Thanks anyway. Take care, Doris.'

'How was the baby?' Frank asked Doris, just before he closed the door.

'Oh Frank, it was covered in poo.'

I got in my car and pulled out my pay-as-you-go phone from my pocket. I had felt it vibrate multiple times during our time in the canteen. Since offing the Mother of Dragons, I hadn't gone back on the suicide forum and had completely forgotten about the phone in my jacket pocket. The screen showed me that I had four messages on www.hangoninthere.com and 1% battery. Shit.

18

Roddy

When Leanne's post-mortem report came back, Dom was clearly impressed with my knowledge and skills, especially when it came to the toxicology report. I could tell this because he only got his phone out twice.

'Similar to the previous report for Graham, it shows that Leanne's cause of death was asphyxiation and there was 0.5% helium detected in the lungs, suggesting that the two of them died the same way,' I read from the report.

'Oh dear, so what do we do now?' Dom asked.

'First of all, we stop saying sissy things like "oh dear" and we go and pay a visit to the mental health therapy group. And, luckily for us, it's on tonight.'

'Actually, I've got a date tonight.'

'No, you don't. Now you've got a date with *me* - not like that though - you might be bent, but I'm not.'

'I'm… not gay, boss.'

'I don't want to know what you do in your spare time, Dom, but if you want to learn about the real world of the police then I suggest you cancel your little date at McDonald's or wherever,' I said, throwing around my authority while mentally deciding that I too would be going to McDonald's for dinner.

We spent the next hour making our way through a box of six glazed donuts and work-shopping possible ways that Graham and Leanne were connected - and how they had both died.

We then moved onto being creative. 'It's called thinking outside the box!' I barked at Dom. We then starting coming up with a few ideas for how to kill each other with helium.

'Maybe they used helium balloons? Easy to get hold of and easy to dispose of.' Dom chirped, which wasn't a totally stupid idea, but I did think that it would probably take quite a bit of balloon sucking to get someone to die.

'What if the helium was a red herring or just a simple coincidence, and the killer used something completely untraceable?' I said excitedly, thinking that I had stumbled across something that was going to break the case wide open.

'But if he used something untraceable, then how are we meant to trace it?' Dom asked, which again wasn't totally stupid.

'True, right… well… ok, so helium was probably used in the death, but how?' I rubbed my chin. *Mmm... still prickly.*

After 20 minutes we had failed to come up with any other way of inhaling helium other than through a tube connected to a helium tank, or through balloons; that's when I decided that it was probably unlikely that Graham and Leanne had died by sucking balloons. Now that we had cleared that up, all we had to do was find where the killer had bought the helium.

We arrived at the nutcase therapy group early so that I could ask the leader, Mitzi (who seemed like the weirdest bird that I'd ever met) for a list of attendees from the past three months. Graham's name didn't appear on the list at all and Leanne's only appeared once. However, there was that other receptionist bird, Sandra. Apparently, she had been attending the group on and off for the past two months.

'She's been coming since she failed to kill herself. It was in the newspaper, so I'm not breaking any doctor-patient confidentiality,' Mitzi explained, winking at me.

'Oh, so you're a doctor!' Dom said, surprised, but the group leader just shook her head.

'Well, a mind and body doctor, but not a medical one. I have no official medical qualifications; I just have a rare gift from mother nature. I should work on you two sometime; your colours are mixed but your moons are in perfect sync,' she said, while waving her hands around and dropping down into the splits.

'You know, I *thought* that our moons were in perfect sync,' Dom chirped, but I just shook my head at him as Mitzi struggled to get up out of the splits.

I informed Mitzi that Dom and I would be staying for the session but that we would be undercover. I told her not to introduce us as the police or ask us anything, which she must have forgotten about, because that's exactly how she introduced me as soon as the session started.

'So, Detective Inspector Roddy... tell us why you're here,' she said, passing along a fluffy teddy. I grew red and my palms started to sweat as I took the teddy and then immediately dropped it to the floor, detective inspectors *do not* hold fluffy teddy bears.

'Strict therapy rules mean that you have to be holding the teddy if you want to speak!' Mitzi spat venomously, with her eyes open wide. I slowly picked the teddy up, not breaking eye contact with the group leader, who was clearly batshit crazy.

I tried my best to think of something to talk about, when suddenly Scottish Mary popped into my head.

'I'm... in love with someone who doesn't love me,' I blurted out.

'Boring!' Mitzi bellowed. 'Tell me something different. Tell me why she doesn't love you and how it depresses you that you can't win over her affection, and really focus on the fact that your colours are fat and boring.'

I was just about to speak when Sandra walked into the hall. She took the spare seat next to Mitzi, hung her coat on the back of the chair, then sat down and looked up to see me staring at her with my mouth wide open. I kept bumping into her. She was at the pub quiz, she was at her flat when I popped round about the helium canister and now she was at the therapy group.

'Excuse me... if you're not going to speak, then please give Mr. Schnitzel to someone else!' Mitzi yelled at me. I realised that I still had my mouth wide open, so I closed it and shook my head with a large grin on my face. Sandra fancied me; there was no other explanation as to why we kept bumping into each other.

'I've tried to win her over, b... but-' I stuttered. I was in love with Mary, but now that Sandra was clearly interested in getting her hands on me, maybe I should pursue her, even if it just made Mary jealous. 'I'm sorry, I've finished my go. Your turn,' I said, throwing the teddy to Dom.

'Right... yeah, well, I've been in my current employment for five years now but I still feel as patronised and micro-managed as I did when I first started -' he began.

He filled up the next 10 minutes telling everyone about how difficult it was to constantly be interrupted and verbally abused by his boss, which by the looks on their faces, no one really cared about.

While Dom was crying like a little bitch, I was busy eyeing everyone up and trying to see which ones looked suicidal - which, to be honest, was all of them. It was obvious to me that although Leanne had been to the group, she had no links to any other members. First of all, she'd only ever been to one meeting and no one worked that quickly. Secondly, no one at the group looked like they had the mental or physical capability to off a poor psycho bint. And lastly, everyone looked like they wouldn't hurt a fly, apart from Mitzi, the group leader - she looked like she'd not only hurt the fly but shout at it and torture it at the same time.

Just before we left the session, I approached Sandra, who seemed to be in a hurry to get out as she was flapping manically to put her coat on.

'Sandra! We must stop running into each other like this. How are you?' I asked her, holding out my hand for her to shake.

RODDY

'Really well, looking forward to doing the superhero balloons for your birthday,' she replied, shaking my hand limply.

'Oh, haha! No they're not for me, they're for my niece. Although maybe I should get you to do my birthday balloons as well, good idea!' I laughed. 'So, I see you've been coming here for a few months now, has it stopped you from wanting to top yourself?'

'Eh...' she looked at me oddly, with her eyebrows in a tight knot, like I had asked her for her bra size or something. 'I'm not going to kill myself,' she said slowly, like she was trying to convince herself rather than me.

'Well, that's *excellent* news! Righto, I shall see you and your balloons in a couple of days,' I said, patting her on the shoulder before spinning on my heels and walking out.

Dom and I made our way to the McDonald's drive-thru to chat about birds and binge on two big macs, three portions of fries, two large milkshakes and four of the new mud pie McFlurries.

'That Sandra woman is odd, isn't she?' Dom said, chomping on his burger while looking through the photos he had discretely taken at the group on his phone. Yes, I suppose she was a bit odd, in a nice way of course. It's funny, because if she wasn't such a lovely person and close friend of Mary's, then I would probably assume that she was involved in the Malford suicides.

'Ha, but that's just silly! The killer is obviously a man,' I said aloud, forgetting that I had been having the first part of that conversation in my head.

19

Roddy

When Dom and I entered the fancy dress shop, we were greeted by a very friendly shop assistant who was dressed as Beetlejuice.

'How can I help you two gentlemen?' Beetlejuice asked, walking around to the other side of the till to greet us.

Suddenly, the shop door burst open, sending the large stack of emoji PEZ dispensers on the counter crashing to the floor.

'Everyone get down! This is a robbery!' shouted a clown in a balaclava, as he came rushing through the door, pointing a gun at Beetlejuice. 'You! Get on the floor *now!*' he screamed.

Dom and I tried out best to hide and keep still behind one of the fancy dress rails, when the clown spotted us and moved his gun to point directly at my face. Something wet and warm started to trickle down my leg.

'Oi, who are you?' he shouted. I shat myself and the smell escaped from my arse quickly. 'Dude, have you just shat yourself?' the clown said, shocked, taking his balaclava off.

Dom, Beetlejuice and I moved slowly to get a good look at the man in the clown outfit; from his clothes, spots and sketchy eyes, he was clearly one of those unemployed druggies that hung out in the park during the day.

'It's not real, it's a water pistol. See?' he said, as he squirted water all over my angry face. I was fuming. 'I just need to bring this pistol back please mate, it's not scary enough for what I need it for,' he said to Beetlejuice as he put the pistol on the counter along with the screwed up receipt from his pocket.

'I dunno, it seemed pretty scary to me,' Beetlejuice laughed, wiping a small tear away from his eyes.

'Shouldn't we arrest him?' Dom whispered to me, but I was too concerned about the fact that I was covered in piss and shit. Today was turning into one of the worst days of my life. All I needed now was for Mary to text me saying that she hated me. My phone buzzed in my pocket and my heart sunk as I took it out. Thankfully, it was just my service provider offering me a better tariff, phew. I turned my phone off and put it back in my pocket.

'Excuse me Beetlejuice, have you sold any helium canisters at all in the last month?' I asked, shuffling towards the counter with my bum clenched and my legs very close together.

'Yes, we sell at least five a day,' he replied, still slightly scared of the drugged-up clown in his shop.

'Five a day, seven days in a week, three weeks in a month. How many canisters is that Dom?' I asked.

'105, but there's four weeks in a-' Dom replied, trying not to look at my messy trousers.

'Exactly. Too many to go through in my opinion. Investigating all those customers would take us on a wild goose chase. Wouldn't you agree Dom?'

'I would.'

'Here's an easier question for you Beetlejuice. Have you had any strange customers in?' I said, looking the clown up and down.

Beetlejuice told me that there was one woman who popped in to buy a helium canister for her triplets' birthdays.

'But I recognized her as that suicide lady out of the paper and they didn't mention any kids in the article,' he informed me.

'Ah yes, that's Sandra. Well, she's just started her own balloon business so that'll be why. Triplets? I don't think she has any kids...?' I wondered.

'No idea, Detective.'

'Me neither,' I said, feeling a little bit of poop slip out of my clenched bum and start to dribble down my leg. 'Well, there's clearly nothing else to investigate here.' Such a pity, I really thought that visiting the main helium canister seller in Malford would have given me some leads, but it had done absolutely nothing - unless that triplet story was of some interest.

'Right, well I'm off to clean myself up and you, dickhead, are never going to pull any pranks like that again because if you do it won't be me shitting myself, it'll be you, through your second arsehole.'

'Got it, sorry, just wanted to bring a little excitement into the world and return the pistol,' the heroin addicted clown said smiling and showing both of his teeth. His red cheeks blushed brighter, almost making him look nervous, but it was probably all the drugs.

'Dom, let's go. This didn't happen,' I said to everyone, as I charged out of the shop and to the safety of my Beemer. My wonderful Beemer that now smelt of McDonald's, piss and shit.

20

Sandra

It was when I was sitting next to the soft drinks table, getting my face painted as a tiger by a five-year old that I realised my life had reached a new low. I had only agreed to blow up sodding balloons for the kids because it got Roddy off my back about the helium canister. I didn't expect to be the children's painting easel and drinks pourer.

My chair was surrounded by packets of unopened character balloons and there was a small helium canister next to me. If it all got too much at the kids' party, I guessed I could always just get my tube out, attach the mask to my face and inhale the stuff right there.

To be honest, I wasn't entirely sure how many kids there were going to be, so I'd brought along 30 balloons, a variation of superheroes, princesses, and puppies; but it turned out that no one was interested in the princesses or puppies.

'I want a Black Panther balloon!' a little girl screamed in my face, as she stomped her feet and clenched her fists.

'Well, I want to be plastered in front of the telly, so we're both out of fucking luck,' I muttered to myself through gritted teeth. Did I mention that I hated social events, kids and pretending to be some sort of balloon extraordinaire? It really brings me out in an angry rash.

Before I had arrived at Roddy's niece's party, I had practised inflating some balloons in my flat. I'd never used helium for anything other than suicides and making my voice sound like Prince, so I needed a bit of practice. I used what was left over from Leanne's canister to practice. Turns out that one medium size helium canister can kill one human and inflate two balloons - value for money or what?

'Did you just say a swear word to Jessica?' a little boy said, running up to me just as I had given the other boy his shit Spiderman balloon.

'Depends, which one is Jessica?'

'The girl with the boy's haircut.'

'Oh her, yeah I did, why… you wanna hear one as well?' The boy nodded his head eagerly, with a huge smile on his face. 'Can you say "bum"?' I whispered to the boy in his ear, but he rolled his eyes and told me that that wasn't a swear word. 'Alright then clever-dick-'

'Clever-dick!' he yelled at the top of his voice.

'Oh shit.'

'Oh shit!' the boy yelled even louder.

'Oh fuck.'

'Oh fu-' I smothered his mouth before he finished, but he wriggled away from me and ran over to his mum. I looked up to the sky and wondered when this hell would end.

When I looked over to the bouncy castle, I saw an angry woman talking to the boy and the boy pointing directly at me. I smiled awkwardly and waved back, trying to seem innocent.

'Excuse me.'

'Holy fuck!' I yelped, as I jumped out of my skin at Roddy, who had come up behind me and put his hand on my shoulder. Me jumping made him jump. 'Yes, what do you want?' I snapped at him.

'Sorry to make you jump, I was just wondering, do you actually like kids?'

'Fuc-,' I took a deep breath, '…no, I'm not the biggest fan of them, why?' I asked.

'I recently heard a rumour that you have triplets,' he said.

'I don't.'

SANDRA

'Didn't think so,' he laughed, 'but I was wondering, could you stop teaching the kids swear words? They're a bit young to be effing and jeffing.'

'It was an accident,' I lied. He held his hands up in surrender and told me that it was fine.

'Accidents happen all the time. You're looking good in that clown outfit by the way,' he winked. As he walked away, he raised an eyebrow flirtingly at me. I wasn't sure whether to puke up a kidney or get up and kick him in the bollocks.

I told the queue of kids that I was going on a break and to come back in ten minutes, to which they all moaned until they saw the big piñata being brought out by one of the mums. My phone buzzed in my pocket as I was busy helping myself to the orange fizzy pop that had been backwashed at least 30 times. I had a new message on the suicide forum. It was from the new user I'd spoken to just the other day; they were asking me whether I had ever known anyone who had gone through with an assisted suicide.

'Why did the elephant leave the circus?' someone asked from behind me. When I turned round, I was greeted by a man with a large red nose, a ghost-like complexion and a party blower in his mouth. Great, another cunting clown. 'Because he was tired of working for peanuts!' The clown in front of me laughed, before blowing the party blower into my face.

'I'm going to give you two seconds to get the *fuck* away from me,' I whispered to him through a fake smile. I was not in the mood for fucking around. 'Also, the elephant is the one called Peanuts, so your joke makes no sense at all.' The clown didn't move, he didn't even drop his smile, nor did he move any further away from me. In fact, my words hadn't seemed to have made any impact on him whatsoever.

'Well, he-*llo*, Mrs. Clown, rawr!' he roared, looking me up and down, 'I normally hate it when I realise there's been a double booking of clowns, but now I'm rather glad.'

'I'm not a clown, I'm the balloon bitch with a tiger painted on my face,' I said, pointing to the packets of balloons on the floor.

Yes, I was wearing a red nose, a yellow hat and had been given shoes that were 10 sizes too big for me, but I was not a sodding clown.

'If you're wondering why the cheeky little parents gave you the clown outfit to wear, that was because I thought that I wouldn't be able to make it, but *voilà*, here I am!'

'Great, I can fuck off then,' I said, before downing my orange fizzy pop and throwing the cup into a large black bin full of half-eaten cake and dog shit, that the owner of the house had forgotten to pick up before everyone arrived.

'Not so fast, tiger lady! I can't do balloons and clown performing at the same time, so you'll have to stay and do the balloons. We'll make a great double act, maybe in more ways than one,' he said, winking at me.

'I'd rather shoot myself point-blank in the face with a rusty shotgun,' I said, sitting back on my seat to get ready for some more balloon inflating.

'Wow, I've never met a woman like you before!'

'Yeah, well there's a lot more where that came from, arseface.'

'You're so insatiable! I want to touch you and make love to you while we're both dressed as clowns,' he said, in between deep, sexual breaths that made me want to puke violently into a child's face.

'I'm being serious - get the fuck out of my face,' I threatened him, as I rose from my chair menacingly. He backed off, but blew me a kiss first.

'Can I have a puppy balloon?' a little boy asked sweetly, pointing at the balloon packet that I had laid out on the floor.

'Please!' I snapped at the boy.

'Please,' he whispered sadly.

'No, I'm on a break,' I told him, getting my phone out of my pocket to check the suicide forum messages again. After thinking about my reply for a good few minutes, I replied to the user explaining, that I did in fact know someone who had died by assisted suicide; and someone who had failed at committing suicide on their own.

I clicked send, put my phone in my pocket and ripped open a puppy balloon packet. As I was inflating the balloon with helium, I noticed Roddy standing over by the bouncy castle. He got his phone out of his jacket pocket, looked around suspiciously and then started to type a text. After a few minutes, he finished typing and put his phone back in his jacket. My phone buzzed violently in my pocket.

21

Roddy

I was having a cracking time at my niece's birthday party, the sun was on my face and I had my third slice of Victoria sponge in my mouth. Over a week ago I had signed up to a suicide forum that I had found on Graham's laptop, and it had been a few days since I'd sent one particular user a message. It had only been a few days since I'd sent the message to DixieDeath5000 but I still hadn't heard anything back and I was getting impatient.

I wanted things to move quicker so that I could get back to filling my day with fun stuff like pissing Dom off and dreaming of Scottish Mary. All Dixie Death needed to do was tell me how people went about organising an assisted suicide, what they did and how they got away with it - simple.

My younger sister had been so busy organising the birthday party that she had almost forgotten to book the balloons. It was lucky that I had popped round to Sandra's when I had, because otherwise we might have had ourselves a balloon-less party. What a cock-up that would've been.

Looking over at Sandra, I felt a bit sorry for her. She was obviously not keen on children as she looked very miserable and seemed to be hating the fact that her face was being painted as a tiger. It was very funny when she had first put on the clown outfit; she had to wear it because our clown had called to say that he was stuck in traffic due to some sort of escaped cow in the road. But it was ok now, because we had a clown, a selection of balloons *and* a bouncy castle.

I hadn't been on a bouncy castle since I was about six years old, so the rainbow unicorn one that my niece was jumping on looked like a lot of bloody fun.

'Right, come on then, let's have a go,' I said to myself as I bent down to take my police boots off. I strutted up to the bouncy castle and watched as all the children ran off the thing and rushed over to their parents. How nice of the kids to let Malford's top police dog have the queer "Unicorn Kingdom" all to himself.

Very slowly and cautiously, I stepped up to the castle with my arms out, trying to find my balance. I walked towards the centre of the unicorn, which I guess would mean that I was standing in its womb. I bent my knees and lifted up, boing, boing, boing, wow… this bouncing thing was fun! Turning around, I waved to all the kids who were looking at me with their mouths wide open. It was nice to see that my bouncing skills were still so impressive.

'Well, don't just stand there, come and join me!' I yelled excitedly in between bounces, but no one seemed to want to join me in the unicorn's womb.

Before I knew it, I was bouncing up high then landing on my bum, then getting up again and bouncing up high to then land on my bum again. Although the bouncy unicorn was fun, it was awfully unstable, because every time I jumped, the whole thing would shake and feel like it was going to collapse.

'Just one more bounce, then I'll get off,' I told my niece, who was frowning hard at me with her little arms crossed and her bottom lip out. With bent knees, I lowered myself as deep as I could, to get as much height from the jump as possible. 'Wheeeeeee!' I laughed, jumping high up into the air, but I had got a little bit too excited, because I leaned forward too much on my way down and ended up landing on my front.

'Oh, my dick!' I cried, as I bounced onto my side and grabbed my crushed manhood. My sister came rushing towards me as a sea of laughter erupted from the children. Then the laughter turned into hissing and the hissing turned into even louder and more violent hissing. The noise seemed to be coming from underneath my crotch area. 'Oh my God, my dick is deflating!'

'Benjamin, don't be so bloody stupid! Your keys have punctured the unicorn - now hold the puncture while I go and get the repair kit.

Once my sister had repaired the hole that my keys had made and I had gone to the toilet to check that my Johnson was ok, I returned to the seat next to the cake table and helped myself to another slice.

The kids all ran back onto the unicorn, but were very quickly told to get off because now that the unicorn was disabled, only three could go on at a time. The others queued up to get a balloon instead.

I'd been watching Sandra inflate the balloons for a little while, when suddenly, I saw poor little tomboy Jessica run away from her and tell her mum something. I then watched as her friend went to speak to Sandra and shouted, "Oh shit!" and "Oh fuck!" at the top of his voice. I got out of my seat and went to talk to her.

'Yes, what do you want?' she snapped at me. She was very ratty for someone who was meant to be a party balloon entertainer; maybe she was on her period.

'Sorry to make you jump love. I was just wondering, do you actually like kids?'

'Fuc-,' she took a deep breath, '...no, I'm not the biggest fan of them, why?'

'I recently heard a rumour that you have triplets,' I said.

'I don't.'

'Didn't think so,' I laughed, 'but I was wondering, could you stop teaching the kids swear words? They're a bit young to be effing and jeffing.'

'It was an accident,' Sandra said. Ah, of course, we all make mistakes. I held my hands up in surrender and told her that it was fine.

'Accidents happen all the time. You're looking good in that clown outfit by the way,' I winked, then walked away, raising one eyebrow flirtingly at her. Even in that stupid clown outfit, she looked seriously shaggable.

If I'm being honest, I still wasn't too sure about Sandra. She seemed very off with me and I wasn't impressed by the swearing, even though it was bloody funny. I wasn't going to say anything else to her about it, but I was going to pop online and do a bit of stalking. But first I quickly popped onto the suicide forum and sent my new pal Dixie Death another message.

I asked them whether they had ever known anyone who had gone through with an assisted suicide and then looked up to see that the originally booked clown had turned up. In fact, by the looks of it, he was busy flirting with Sandra because they were standing awfully close. My mind quickly jumped to imagining the two of them shagging in clown outfits; quite scary but quite sexy as well.

I took another slice of cake and went to join my sister next to the queer bouncy castle, to make sure she hadn't heard about the whole swearing incident with the kids. She told me that yes, of course she had heard the swearing and she wasn't best pleased, but she didn't want to make a fuss, so she was just going to leave a bad review for her business online. I turned back around and saw Sandra on her mobile, while there was a queue of kids in front of her waiting for their balloons. She put her phone in her top pocket and ripped open another balloon packet. My phone buzzed in my pocket.

It was funny really, because it looked for a second there like Sandra was the one who was messaging me. But it wasn't her, it was Dixie Death, finally. They said that they did know someone who had died by assisted suicide - brilliant, I wondered whether Dixie Death was involved at all. As I sent my reply asking for more details on how to do it and how to make sure that no one found out, I noticed Sandra stuff the balloon into the child's hand and then get her own phone out again.

This really was turning out to be the oddest coincidence. If she wasn't such a snappy, hormonal bitch, I would've gone over and told her about it. I'm sure she'd find it funny.

Taking no time at all, it looked like she had typed something short and sweet before putting her phone back in her pocket, but at the same time that she did, my phone buzzed in my pocket again. I had a short message from Dixie Death, asking why I was so interested. So, I quickly replied saying that I was suicidal and needed some help killing myself. I tried my best not to laugh. Me? Suicidal? What a joke!

I told myself that if Sandra got her phone out again after I sent the message, then it might be more than just a coincidence. I sent the message. Two seconds later, she reached into her pocket.

22

Sandra

The divorce had finally gone through and I planned to celebrate my freedom from that fuckwit, by getting absolutely shitfaced. Fortunately, on that same day, I had been invited round to visit one of my old regular patients, Doris, and her husband Frank for dinner and a few bottles of wine. Unfortunately, I was still having to drive to a newsagent outside of Malford to get said wine; thanks, Mother.

'I'm here to celebrate,' I said, when Doris opened the door to see me standing there with three bottles of wine and a bunch of flowers balanced in my arms.

'Lovely Dear! We've just bought some new sherry and Frank is playing Barry Manilow on the piano. We'll have a little old-fashioned piano party,' Doris said, quietly kissing me on the cheek and welcoming me inside. I liked old people; they were friendly and less cuntish than other people, but their houses always smelt the same; musky with a hint of death.

'To divorce', I raised my glass after finishing my food, 'and to your very happy 59 years of beautiful marriage,' I slurred, as we all clinked glasses. The smoked salmon with cream cheese and selection of buffet nibbles had been eaten to the tunes of "Mandy", "Copacabana" and Frank's famous "Manilow Medley". I'd drunk most of the wine that I'd brought, while Doris had had just one thimbleful of her new sherry.

At half eleven, I decided that it was time to go home and leave my elderly friends to go to bed.

'We've not been up this late since 1984 dear. It makes a nice change, doesn't it, Frank?' Doris said to Frank, who had stopped playing the piano half an hour ago and was slumped over, asleep on the stall.

'Are you sure you don't want to stay, dear?'

'No, honestly it's fine. I'll be a horror in the morning. I'll walk back to my place; it's only 10 minutes away.' I gave Doris a hug before grabbing my coat off the hook and opening the front door.

I said my goodbyes and walked down the street towards my flat. It was only a mile away and because I was absolutely smashed, it felt like it was just around the corner. As I walked down the road, I saw a little cat playing with its tail on the floor. I bent down and stroked it.

'Hello, little kitty.'

'Sandra!'

'Fuck me, it speaks.' I said, alarmed at the cat, but then I heard Frank call my name again and I stood up and turned back, drunkenly looking at Frank, confused. He'd been fast asleep just a few seconds ago.

'You finally woke up then, Frank?' I laughed, stumbling back to the house to give him a hug goodbye.

'It's Doris, she's collapsed!' he shrieked.

I rushed back into the house and found Doris lying on the floor. I called 999 and an ambulance arrived four minutes later. The sight of the ambulance's interior triggered a heavy black cloud in my mind. I had been in and out of consciousness when I had been bundled into the back of that same vehicle after I'd overdosed, and the memory of that time sobered me up quicker than any greasy fry-up could ever do.

Doris was rushed into the A&E department at Malford Hospital, followed by a terrified Frank - and me, still a bit shitfaced, but still not the most shitfaced I'd ever been at work. Doris regained consciousness half an hour after arriving at the hospital and was quickly whisked away to the MRI machine to see what had caused her temporary blackout.

Frank and I comforted Doris as she laid on the hospital bed with a hot cup of tea, while we waited for her results.

'Why don't you go home Dear? Frank is here, you go and get some rest,' Doris said, smiling at me. I ignored her, propped up her pillows and rearranged her blanket to ensure it was fully covering her legs.

'Honestly, it's fine. I want to stay here and make sure that you're alright. Plus, I might book this in as overtime to help pay for the divorce,' I said, looking over to Frank, who was asleep again, this time in a chair, still holding onto Doris' hand.

It was another two hours before the doctor came back to deliver the results of her scan. The doctor revealed that she had a brain tumour the size of a ping-pong ball and that they needed to investigate it further before they could give a proper diagnosis.

Eventually, I jumped into a taxi and made my way home. A week later, the diagnosis came, and you could say it wasn't the best news; secondary cancer that had metastasised from the colon. She didn't have long left.

23

Sandra

It had been three weeks since I'd become a mother to five guinea pigs, and two weeks since the old-fashioned piano party where Doris had collapsed. I'd been texting the suicide forum user a little bit, but as I wanted to calm things down, I was only very vague.

When I'd found out that Doris had terminal secondary cancer, I'd gone round to hers bearing flowers and chocolates. Frank ushered me into their house and took me upstairs, to see Doris, sat up in bed, dressed in a lime green dressing gown and eating toast. From the strained look on her face, she was clearly in a great deal of pain.

We sat either side of the bed while she asked how I was, how work had been and what the cure for cancer was. She'd been told that she'd have maybe seven months left if she accepted treatment, or two months if she didn't. Unfortunately, she had completely dismissed the idea of any treatment.

Even after two hours of my best convincing speech, I couldn't persuade her to go through with it. I can very much appreciate the irony of me trying to convince someone to accept treatment to prolong their life, when I had been busy shortening the lives of no fewer than three people within the last two months.

'What do you think about this, Frank?' I asked.

'I don't want to lose her,' he said sadly, taking hold of Doris's hand and smiling at her, '...but I don't want her to be in any pain.'

SANDRA

Frank told me that what he was most scared of was seeing his beloved wife die in agony. Doris said that she wasn't scared of death; it was just that she also didn't want to be in agony, especially as she had heard stories from the other ladies at the WI that had terrified her.

Friends, who had been in so much pain that they were begging for death. If she went before the pain kicked in, then she would be happy. Well, she wouldn't be happy because she'd be dead, but her ghost would be happy.

'We even asked if they had anything stronger than morphine to make me comfortable, but the nice doctor sadly said no,' she said, still smiling her sweet smile.

This would be the perfect time to start reeling off my suicide speech, but that was definitely not what I was going to do here. Rule number two of Sandra's assisted suicide scheme: Don't do it to anyone I know.

'Help me make some tea, would you dear?' Frank asked me, as he slowly let go of Doris's hand and walked out of the room. We slowly made our way downstairs and into the kitchen, where I filled up the kettle and turned on the switch. Frank switched the kettle off at the plug, lowered his head to his chest and leaned his body awkwardly against the countertop. We stood in silence for a couple of minutes.

'I'm absolutely devastated,' he said, eventually raising his head up.

'I can't begin to comprehend what you are going thr-' I started to say.

'I need your help. We both need your help.' He had interrupted me, which I was willing to overlook but just as a note, I fucking hate being interrupted.

'I'm just the receptionist; there's nothing that I can do that the oncologist can't,' I told him, even though I had a huge bloody feeling that he wasn't asking me to help convince her to go through with treatment.

'That's not what I meant. I don't know if you have any access to anything that may ease Doris's pain...' Frank said.

'Something like Morphine?' I asked.

'No.'
'Tramadol?'
'Nope.'
'Codeine?'
'No.'
'Aspirin?'
'No.'
'Ibuprofen?'
'No.'
'Paracetamol?'
'Do you think I don't know how to go to the shop and buy paracetamol, dear?'
'You don't mean any painkillers, do you?'
'No. I mean something that is going to help her on a more permanent basis. I don't know if he told you, but Graham was a friend of mine.'
Oh fuck. How the hell did he know Graham and why the hell was he bringing him up? My heart sank and my eyes closed.
'He told you about me?'
'Yes dear,' he replied.
'I see.'
The next day at work, I tried my best to put Doris and Frank to the back of my mind and focus on my breathing, just like crazy, LSD-loving Mitzi had taught me.

To celebrate Ursula returning to work after her ridiculously spontaneous Caribbean holiday, she and I had ordered some posh salads from Malford's health food cafe to eat in the staff room. Joining us was Rosie from paediatrics, who had popped out to buy a McDonald's. 367 holiday photos later, Ursula was still trying to convince us both that she hadn't booked the impulsive holiday just so that her husband wouldn't go on the stag do.

'Come on ladies, I wouldn't take my husband on an impulsive all-expenses-paid holiday just so that he wouldn't go on a stag do, where he might or might not sleep with someone else and completely ruin

SANDRA

both our lives. I'm just not that sort of person,' Ursula said, sipping her tea with her pinky up.

'To be fair though, your husband is proper fit,' Rosie said.

'Thank you, Rosie,' Ursula said, rolling her eyes and staring out the window. 'So, you're officially divorced now are you Sandi?' she asked. I nodded as I finished eating my egg salad.

'Yup, he's gone and hopefully I'll never see him again. But knowing Oliver, like I do, I'm sure he'll pop round at least once a day to tell me that he still loves me. Oh, and Claire is pregnant, so there's also that,' I said.

Rosie scoffed her McDonald's fries while telling me how unfit Oliver was and how she couldn't imagine us banging.

'I just keep thinking that he'd be all limp and the whole thing would look a bit shit really!' Rosie laughed.

'Thanks, Rosie,' I said, staring at her with one eyebrow raised. If I could've been bothered, I would've been offended by her words, but I really couldn't give a fuck. Also, I'm sure I do look a bit shit when I'm shagging, I like to just lay there.

'No problem doll, it's good that you got rid of him. Now we can set you up with someone proper buff. I'm thinking of breaking up with one of my boyfriends; you can have him! Oh shit, is that the time?' Rosie said, chucking the rest of the fries in her mouth and hurrying out of the staff room.

Once Rosie had gone, Ursula asked me about my balloon business.

'So how did you get into it?' she asked, delicately positioning some lettuce onto her fork.

'Well, I needed more money and I like balloons, so I thought, "why not combine the two and sell balloons?"' I replied, trying my best to stretch my mouth into a convincing smile.

'Listen Darling, I know you've been going through a hard time, but I really don't believe you at all. Balloons? Guinea pigs? Listen, you can talk to me, sweetie. What's going on?' she asked, tilting her head to the side, concerned. Should I tell Ursula about what I had done to

Graham, Leanne and the Mother of Dragons? Maybe I could just tell her what Frank had asked me to do. It might give me some clarity on the situation and help make up my mind.

Since we had known each other, Ursula had always had my back and had always been supportive of any decision that I had made, apart from when I chose to overdose. Even though she had hated me for doing it, she had still been unbelievably supportive in the aftermath.

Deep down, I knew that I wanted to help Doris, but I also knew that I couldn't risk talking to Ursula about it in case she told someone.

'So, are you and Alec having an affair or are you just touching each other tenderly at parties?' I asked, boldly popping a piece of egg into my mouth. It was obvious that some sort of bollocks was going on between them, and if I made her focus on that, then she would stop asking me about my pretend balloon business.

24

Roddy

As soon as I'd found out that Sandra was the Dixie Death user that I'd been messaging on the suicide forum, I'd been keeping a very close eye on her. I'd driven past her work multiple times; this may or may not have been because I could also get a glimpse of Mary at the same time. I'd also sat outside her flat and watched people come and go, but no one had taken any helium canisters inside. It was obvious that Sandra was going to be the next victim in this sick suicide club, because she was on the same forum that Graham had been on. Oh, and also she had already tried to kill herself once.

In order to save Sandra from death, I had to find the killer before they got to her. Dom and I made ourselves busy by going through Graham and Leanne's laptops and mobile phones again to double check if they had had any contact with each other, or if they had someone in common. So far, the only number that came up in both Graham and Leanne's mobile phone records was Kebaby's, the local - and only - kebab shop in Malford.

Funnily enough, I had visited that exact kebab shop just the night before, on my way home from a rather rubbish night of trying to woo Scottish Mary at the quiz.

'Large chicken doner shish kebaby!' I had shouted drunkenly over the counter at the very sober and bored looking man. 'Oi oi, don't turn around, I haven't finished. Extra-large cheesy chips on the side.'

I wiggled my hand drunkenly in the air while leaning on the shop counter.

The bored man handed me a large chicken kebab and chips along with my change, but I waved the change away giving it to the man as a tip. I'm a giver like that.

'I'm a detective inspector by the way,' I said smugly, turning around.

'I'm a trained lawyer from Syria escaping my war-torn country by the way,' the man had replied, but I was too busy chomping happily on my kebab to reply.

'Really delicious kebab it was too!' I told Dom, as I started to salivate at the thought of it. Dom ignored me and continued to nose his way around Graham's laptop. He found some badly-taken photos of farmyard animals and I found a large number of torrented films and music on Leanne's laptop. What a crook!

We had both been through the post-mortem and toxicology reports numerous times and had tried our best to investigate the case. It also seemed that none of the family members knew anything about Graham's depression and the only friend that Leanne had, had said that she wasn't really surprised that she had chosen to kill herself.

'We just need someone else to die - but not Sandra - so that we can start joining the dots and make a pyramid like they do on Line of Duty. At the moment, we've just got a line...' I said, proving my point by drawing a line between the picture of Leanne and Graham that I had stuck up on the wall.

'Maybe the next victim could be an old, black man so we had a bit more diversity,' Dom suggested.

'I don't think there are any old black men in Malford. There's Femidom but he's not old... well, he might be actually; they say "black don't crack."'

'They also say something else about black men-'

'Don't be disgusting, Dom.'

25

Sandra

Since Frank had subtly asked me to help bump Doris off, I had thought of nothing else. Well, apart from Oliver, but that was just because he hadn't stopped texting, asking me how I was doing. Eventually, I had to block him. If only I could help *him* hop off this mortal coil.

I really did like helping kill people who were messed up in the head. But this was very different; I was fond of Doris and Frank and would be less able to live with myself than I already was now. Perhaps I could make a deal with myself; if I helped Doris on her way to the party in the sky, then I would never do it to anyone else again. But then what else would I do with my life?

Even with this deal in my mind, my gut still told me not to bloody do it. But could I live with myself if I knew that Doris was suffering, and Frank was trapped, watching the rapid demise of his soulmate? Probably, but I'd rather not. At that moment, a sweet old man knocked on my door.

'Frank, I've already said I won't do it,' I said, staring at Frank, who was holding a bunch of flowers and wearing a small pleading smile on his face.

'Won't do what, dear?'

'You want me to,' I lowered my voice, '...help Doris, you know, be "permanently comfortable."' Frank stepped into my apartment, gripping his bunch of flowers too tightly and shaking a little.

'Oh, I'm not here for that, dear,' he said as I shut the door.

'Oh, ok great. Well, thank you for the flowers,' I said, moving towards them with my hand out. Frank pulled them away quickly.

'They aren't for you! And of course that's why I'm here. Oh, you have guinea pigs!' he chuckled, pointing to the guinea pigs that were running around in the big dog cage that I'd bought them, the little one that I'd taken from the Mother of Dragons' house having been far too small.

The flowers were for Doris, of course. She had received so many flowers since her diagnosis that she could open her own Interflora franchise. Obviously, she wouldn't live long enough to really get the business going though, and by that time all the flowers would have died. Probably her too.

'I want to do what's best for my wife. We've had an amazing life together, you see.'

Unbeknownst to Frank, he was wasting his time trying to convince me with memories and stories from their past about his time during the war, and how he had come back just to marry Doris. Their adventures on holidays, their decision not to have children - although they both loved their goddaughter - and their passionate sex life that had gone on well into their 80s. I'd already made up my mind that I would do this last thing for Doris, but I didn't tell Frank straight away; his reminiscing put a huge smile on his face and it seemed mean to end it.

Frank left with the smile on his face and a tear in his eye. He would be able to help his wife with the biggest challenge that they would ever face. He had assured both Doris and I that he would grieve for the rest of his life, but that he would also take a huge amount of comfort that she was in heaven waiting for him. I didn't have the heart to tell him that heaven was a load of bollocks and Doris would only be waiting in the ground for him. I thought it was a bit cruel to tell him that.

Due to Doris denying treatment, her condition was deteriorating fast, so I had to act quickly. I only had enough supplies for one last job; it was lucky that Frank hadn't wanted to go too, as he would've been shit out of luck. Once I had helped Doris, I thought about going to Florence and jumping off one of the bridges, after taking an extremely liberal dose of sleeping tablets, codeine and those antidepressants that I'd been prescribed but hadn't bothered taking.

It was going to be beautiful and fucking tragic at the same time; just me, the sun and an Italian bridge. One, two, three... and jump. I would definitely be successful this time, as the combination of jumping off a bridge and downing a huge cocktail of drugs would certainly be a lethal one.

When I had first discovered the suicide bag, I had decided that I would use that technique to kill myself, but I had changed my mind for two reasons. 1) Because I wanted to die somewhere beautiful and not in my miserable bloody flat and 2) Because, call me soft, but I didn't think it was very nice to let the people you're closest to, to find you dead while hooked up to a helium canister.

26

Roddy

We were about to give up surveillance on Sandra, when we saw an old bloke walk up to the block of flats, holding a bunch of flowers.

'Hey up, what's this?' I said excitedly, sitting up properly in the car seat.

'Looks like an elderly man, boss.'

'Yes, I can see that,' I snapped.

'Then why did you ask me what it was, boss?'

'Do you want to be on desk duty, Dom?'

'I already am, boss.'

'Then what are you doing in the car with me, doing secret surveillance for then?'

'You said you wanted company, boss.'

'Oh yeah. Well… don't get any funny ideas, alright? I just get bored on my own sometimes; I'm not a faggot.'

'Of course not, boss, you've just spent the last two hours talking about Scottish Mary's sexy body.'

Ah yes, Scottish Mary… *'God, I'd bloody love to bang her,'* I thought. She wasn't the hottest bird in the world and she was one of those dykes, but there was something quite special about her that just made me lose my mind. The days in between our weekly meetings at the pub quiz dragged slowly and I would find myself thinking of nothing else.

'We should go and see Mary!' I burst out.

'Shall we see who this elderly man is first, boss?'

'Good idea, but then we'll question Mary on her friend and see if she can give us something.'

'Like some food?'

'What?!'

'Nothing, sorry boss. The hunger is going to my head.'

'We'll get food in a minute. Let's see what this dirty old man is up to. He could be her bit of fun on the side.'

'On the side of what? I thought we found out yesterday that she's recently divorced,' Dom said, getting his camera out.

'I can't really imagine an old bloke banging, can you?'

'I try not to, boss,' Dom replied, taking a picture of the old man pressing the buzzer to Sandra's flat.

I decided that we would wait for the old codger for 30 minutes and then bomb it to the hospital to see Scottish Mary.

'What do you think of that black Mercedes over there?' I asked Dom, who was taking pictures of Sandra through her front window.

'It's ok, boss. Do you think it's dodgy?'

'No, I think it looks sexy. Do you think it's sexier than this BMW?'

'I don't think cars look sexy at all, boss. I've got a bicycle.'

'Ha! Bicycle! Of course you have.'

'You've seen me on it, boss.'

'Have I?'

'Yes, boss, when you tried to run me over.'

'No I didn- Is that him finished already?' I exclaimed, pointing at the old bloke walking out of the block of flats with the flowers he had brought with him. 'So, he brought Sandra some flowers but then didn't give them to her.'

'Maybe their meeting didn't go very well, or perhaps they weren't for her in the first place.'

'Mmm, maybe...'

When we arrived at the hospital, Scottish Mary was busy dealing with what looked like an emergency patient, but I told her that I needed to see her urgently and that the bloke with the bleeding wound would have to wait.

Mary took Dom and I into a private room where we could ask her some questions related to our suicide investigation.

'Don't you need to deal with that patient first?' Dom asked her.

'Are you a hospital receptionist?' she asked him.

'No, I'm not but -'

'Right well don't tell me how to do my job and I won't tell you how to do yours.' She winked at him.

Unfortunately, we only got to ask Mary a few questions about what she knew about the suicides before the German head of the hospital burst into the room and told Mary to get back to the desk.

'Listen here, you Jerry-'

'It's Leonard, boss,' Dom whispered to me.

'Listen here, Leonard boss. I can arrest you for obstructing the course of justice.'

'Oh dear, can you?' he laughed, '...well, you do that and Mary, you finish up with that bleeding man outside. If you want to question a receptionist, you can have one who isn't currently on shift for another ten minutes. Sandra, *geh jetzt in den raum.*'

In stepped Sandra who still had her coat and bag on. She had clearly just walked into the hospital. Leonard smiled and tried his best to quickly usher a slow, annoyed Mary down the corridor.

'What can I help you with?' Sandra asked, standing by the door with her arms folded.

'Well, Dixie Death...' I paused, trying to read her reaction, but she kept her face still, '...how about you tell us why you were on that suicide forum. And also how you got from your flat to here so bloody quickly.'

'Which one would you like to know first?' She asked.

'The one about why you're on a suicide forum.'

'Because my father committed suicide, I tried to commit suicide and someone in Malford recently committed suicide, so you could say that I have an interest in suicide,' she said, not moving from the door.

'Interesting. So why did you delete your profile yesterday?'

'I had someone messaging me that I didn't feel comfortable about. I'm guessing that was you?'

A small laugh masked as a cough escaped from Dom's mouth. I gave him a thump under the table and resumed my composure.

'Yes, that was me. I was worried about you, I *am* worried about you.'

'Why?' Sandra asked, screwing up her face. Finally, a reaction.

'Because I don't know how much you know about what's been going on, but we seem to have a suicide killer in Malford.' Dom coughed again.

'A suicide killer?' Sandra raised one eyebrow.

'Someone is going around killing the good people of Malford and making it look like suicide. So naturally, when I discovered it was you on the suicide forum, I was worried. Any friend of Mary's is a friend of mine and I wouldn't want anything to happen to you.'

She stood there, thinking for a few moments before replying.

'That's, um, sweet of you, but I think I'll be fine. As much as I'd like to hang out with you two, I've got ill people to check in to their appointments.'

'Just be careful,' I said.

'I will,' She replied. She went to open the door but then she froze and turned to look at me again. 'Do you have any suspects yet?'

'We do have a suspect in mind, yes. So, like I said, be careful.' I winked at her.

'Do we have a suspect in mind, boss?' Dom asked, when Sandra had left.

'That we do, Dom. That we do.'

27

Sandra

After Roddy had told me that he had a suspect in mind for the killer suicides and then had winked at me like a fucking creep, I went to distract my anxiety by talking to Irish Jenny in the bowel ward.

'Well, I'll tell ya, before I had the operation, my poo was orange in colour.' Irish Jenny laughed as she sucked noisily on a boiled sweet. Her operation had gone well, and she was finally on the road to recovery. Her mystery daughter still hadn't paid a visit yet and Jenny said that if she didn't before she was discharged in two days, then she would write her out of her and her husband's will.

'Who will you leave everything to then?' I asked, not really caring.

'I might leave it to the donkey sanctuary. Not because I want the donkeys to have it, I mean, what are they going to do with the money? Go on a bloody donkey spa weekend? I only want to give it to the donkeys because my daughter hates them, so it'll be a double burn.' This, I imagined, was another lie. I mean, who has any strong feelings towards donkeys? Hateful or otherwise.

'I went on a cruise once,' Irish Jenny said randomly, smiling to herself at what was clearly a happy memory. 'I threw one of the other passengers overboard because they were annoying me. They were never found and no one ever suspected me.' She looked at me with a weird expression on her face. 'I've never told anyone that before. Oh dear, you won't say anything will you?'

'Um, no?' I said slowly, not believing her. 'How did they annoy you?'

'John and I had made some friends on the boat and then the bloke kept interrupting everyone, answering questions that someone had asked me... and I didn't like his face. His wife didn't really like him either, so I thought I'd throw him overboard one evening when it was just us out on the deck. I told everyone that he'd fallen overboard and after they finished the search for him, the three of us enjoyed the rest of our cruise. I didn't mean to kill him; I just wanted him to shut the hell up, ya know?' she said, shrugging her shoulders as if to say, "Hey ho."

Later on that day, I asked her husband John about it and he said that she had told a few porkies in her life, but that was one of the biggest ones. He said that they hadn't even been on a cruise; it was just that now she was older, she liked making up stories to see other people's reactions. In recent years, she had also taken up petty theft from shops, but just silly things like socks, mars bars or small electrical goods that hadn't been hooked up to any sort of security system. Sounds quite thrilling, after this suicide thing ends I might think of taking that up myself.

The time that I had been dreading came around quickly. After getting home from work, I packed my suitcase full of the necessary essentials, including my last helium canister, before trying my best to go into autopilot mode and drive towards Doris's house.

Taking the long way made me later than I'd said I would be, but I needed the time to clear my head. I parked one road away, locked my car and walked towards the house, holding my small suitcase handle tightly. Doris and Frank's front door opened, and a tall blonde lady walked out, saying what seemed to be an emotional goodbye. I began to panic. Had they told someone that I was helping her commit suicide? Had she told her my name? Where I worked? My shoe size? Ok, probably not the last one, but my doubts were now red fucking hot, giving me a tight feeling in my chest.

First of all, I'd never wanted to help Doris, (see rule number two: don't do it to anyone I know) and now that there was a possibility that they had told someone else, someone else who could very easily go to the police station and report me. Yes, they were old, sweet and seemed like trustworthy people, but Graham had seemed trustworthy and he had told his friend Frank what I'd done.

The blonde lady walked down the pathway, smiling at Doris and waving to her before closing the gate and immediately starting to walk towards me. I was only two houses away when we walked past each other, and we made eye contact. She was a very hot woman with long legs and a gorgeous model-like face. In fact, she was so beautiful that it was almost offensive. I gripped my suitcase handle even tighter and considered walking back around the block to where I'd parked my car and driving the fuck away.

'Sandra, dear!' Doris called out weakly from the front door as I passed the house. I shook off my concentration and looked up to see Doris and Frank giving me the same confused look that the hot blonde lady had.

'Oh, hi Doris! I didn't see you there. How are you?' I said, walking cheerily up their pathway while trying my best to look like I was pleasantly surprised to see Doris, rather than absolutely fucking horrified.

When the front door shut, I let go of my suitcase, dropped my pretend smile and stared at Doris and Frank, who were smiling at me by the front door.

'Who was that? What have you told her? If you've mentioned anything about me, I'm sorry, but I won't be able to go ahead with it. I want to do this for you Doris, but, but, I just can't risk being put in prison. I just can't,' I stuttered.

A very clear image of what was going to happen sped through my mind. I would kill Doris, the blonde woman would tell the police that she had seen a mysterious woman enter their house and the police would eventually discover that the mysterious woman was me. The police would then arrive at the hospital and I would quickly rush to my car and drive back to my flat. But I would be followed by the police, who would chase me out of my flat, making me run as fast as I could, which was not fucking fast at all. I'd end up on the bridge where I'd met Graham, and after half an hour of the police trying to talk me down, I would jump.

I'd smack the water at 100 miles an hour, but I wouldn't die, I'd end up paralysed from head to toe, be found guilty of the murder of Graham, the Mother of Dragons, Leanne and Doris and spend the rest of my life either in a hospital prison or in my mother's villa. If I chose my mother's villa, then I'd spend my days listening to and watching my mother parade around with Miguel and other young floozy men, while not being able to do anything about it. I would have to rely on Mum to feed, clean and look after me. It would be torture.

Frank put a warm, comforting hand on my shoulder as I took a deep breath, and he reassured me that they hadn't told Selena, (the hot blonde had a name). She was just their goddaughter who they'd had round for dinner, because Doris wanted to see her one last time.

'Then why the emotional goodbye with all the hugs and sad looks?' I asked.

'She's an emotional person. She's not English, so she's more in touch with her feelings, that's all.' The three of us sat down in the kitchen with a cup of tea and biscuits. I took three - I needed the sugar.

Tea, perfect for any occasion, whether you're sitting in the garden, in a restaurant or in someone's kitchen about to kill them. It's always so perfect. Good old English fucking tea.

Doris and Frank had had a while to prepare to say their goodbyes and Doris told me that she'd invited so many close family members and friends round for dinner in the past few weeks, that people almost suspected something. She said that she hadn't told them about the cancer, but she had found it hard to hide the pain.

Eventually, we made our way upstairs and I waited outside the bedroom as Doris put on her old lady nightie and got into bed. When

I eventually walked into the bedroom, I saw that Frank had also put on his night clothes and had gotten into the bed with his wife. I hoped he didn't think that I was helping him as well because he was out of luck. I only had the one canister and there was nothing wrong with him, apart from being a fan of Barry Manilow.

'Are you ready, my beautiful?' Frank said, kissing Doris's hand as he tried to hold back a tear that was threatening to fall down his face.

'I'm ready, sweetheart.' They kissed. It was sweet, but then they didn't stop for ages. They kept kissing - it was wet and passionate and long. Jesus Christ, I'd never kissed anyone like that before. Wow, they were really going at it. Frank pushed his body nearer to Doris's and for a second, I thought they were going to have one last shag.

Luckily, they eventually stopped snogging like horny teenagers and I quietly set Doris up with the gel, the mask and the tube that was attached to the canister.

After I had done my business, I waited downstairs in the kitchen, allowing Frank some private time with his wife as she slowly slipped away from him. An hour later, I walked up the stairs to find Frank sorrowfully staring at his wife. She looked like she was asleep.

I felt for her pulse, but it wasn't there. She was gone. I carefully removed the mask and cleaned her face gently with the wipes from my suitcase.

'She's in a better place now,' I said, sitting down on the bed next to Frank, who sat up a bit, still holding Doris's hand tightly. I didn't really believe in an afterlife, but I hoped that if it did exist then it really was a better place. But for all I knew, it could be a real shithole; somewhere like Peckham, perhaps.

'She's is at peace now,' Frank said, smiling down at her gently, stroking her cheek. He turned to me with a sad look on his face and said, 'I want to go with her.'

Time seemed to slow down, I didn't answer him. Instead, I just stared at him for a while as I thought about it.

'I can't,' I muttered slowly. I wasn't sure if there would be enough helium left in the tank for him and I didn't want to risk it going wrong and something worse happening.

'I thought you might say that. I was going to ask you before, but I couldn't risk Doris finding out. She had enough on her plate,' Frank sighed, as he looked sweetly at his dead wife.

'It's not that I don't want to help you join Doris. It's that I don't know if I have enough stuff left. I could come back tomorrow,' I suggested, running out of ideas. But I was rather hoping that he would say, "No, don't be silly."

'No, tomorrow won't do. It has to be tonight.' I got up and started pacing around the room, trying to think of what I could do. 'When we were fighting in Paris in the 40s, a buddy and I came across this very beautiful looking gun on the floor and we took it. I remember that gun, it saved me many times during that war. Oh, the stories I could tell you.' He smiled to himself, and his skin crinkled heavily around his eyes, which were wet with tears. 'Still, there's no time for stories now.' I stood, frozen, listening to Frank. 'I want to thank you from the bottom of my heart for helping Doris and me. You will never know how grateful we are.' Talk about guilt tripping me. I didn't want to kill Frank as well, but now I felt that I didn't really have a choice.

'I could try and get some more supplies now if you just give me an hour,' I said, feeling slightly irritated at the inconvenience.

'It's ok, Dear.' He smiled. With his hand still tightly holding onto Doris's, he used his other hand to open his bedside drawer and take out the gun that he had found all those years ago. He put the muzzle in his mouth slowly and calmly, and pulled the trigger.

28

Sandra

I stood there for what seemed like hours, my hand covering my mouth, in complete shock at seeing Frank shoot himself just a few feet away from where I was standing.

'Oh fuck!' My body shook hard from shock. 'Oh fuck!' I'd thought that finding my dad hanging would be the worst thing that I'd see in my life, but it wasn't. My heart felt like it had exploded and I couldn't avert my eyes. He was dead, alright. She was dead and that had been fairly easy to deal with, but now he was dead, and his brains were dripping down the ancient yellowing wallpaper like thick, gloopy ketchup.

I had to think quickly. Being an old gun, the shot had been very loud and the neighbours, although probably fairly aged, had probably heard it. I grabbed my stuff and headed downstairs while quickly checking myself in the hallway mirror to make sure that there wasn't any blood splatter on me.

Ignoring the want to stay and cry for the two lovely people who were lying upstairs, dead, I got the hell out of the house.

The darkness was thick as I closed the front door quietly and shuffled quickly along the pavement. Further down the road, a black Audi was parked, but I couldn't see the number plate because it had its lights on. It could've been the same one that had been outside of my flat, but I thought that the Audi was the least of my fucking worries at that moment. I ignored it and continued to race towards my car.

When I reached my Volvo, I drove to the nearest Tesco and spent a long time shopping, ensuring that every CCTV camera in the shop saw and recorded me. If I had an alibi for the night that the two deaths had happened, then I couldn't be suspected of having any involvement.

But I was still shaking from shock as I reached out for a bag of guinea pig food, nearly dropping it on the floor. This one would be all over the news; more than Leanne's and Graham's death had been. It was bound to be investigated by more than just the local idiot detective.

'No, I don't need any help packing,' I said to the checkout assistant, who blew a large bubble of gum in response. 'How's your evening going?' I asked, trying to get some conversation going so that she would remember me just in case the CCTV system was down. Normally I hated making small talk with shop assistants, but this time it was important.

The checkout assistant just chewed her gum and looked at me.

'I've just come from that amazing new bar in town, do you know it?' I lied, manically packing frozen and cosmetic items into the same bag like an absolute psycho. A new bar hadn't opened in Malford for over 20 years, but I thought that young people liked bars, so maybe that would get her talking.

'What? Who does their weekly shopping when they're drunk?' she asked, reeking of attitude and boredom. I found it funny that she thought that my 15 random items were the contents of a weekly shop.

'No, I'm not drunk; I drove here,' I laughed, trying to stop my hands from shaking so much.

'You've been drink driving? My cousin did that, then he was banned for like three years or whatever, but he still drove. His girl had to get to the hospital to have his kid, so how else was he supposed to get there?'

'Well, exactly,' I agreed, not paying the slightest bit of attention.

'I'm afraid if you've been drinking and you plan on driving, I'm going to have to refuse to serve you and immediately call the pigs,' she said in between gum bubbles.

'No, you can serve me. I'm not even buying any alcohol and I'm not drunk. I've never drunk alcohol and driven, ever.'

'I'm going to have to get the supervisor. Supervisor!' the checkout assistant yelled at the top of her voice, while buzzing the bell under the till as if she'd gone berserk.

The checkout assistant and I stared at each other, while we waited for the supervisor to finish his fag and sort out this issue, that was not an issue at all. In fact, it was the most non-issue issue ever. The assistant blew a large bubble and continued to chew and stare with serious teenage attitude, until the supervisor eventually showed up.

'What's the problem, Destiny?' the supervisor asked, as he wiped the cigarette ash off his fleece.

'She's been drink driving and I'm refusing to serve her.'

'I haven't been drinking! I plan to do a lot of drinking once I get home, but I haven't had anything since last night. Please just serve me and we can all get on with our dull, boring lives,' I said, with tightly crossed arms that just wouldn't stop fucking shaking.

'Destiny, stop being so stupid and serve the woman,' the man said, before holding out a tissue for her to reluctantly put her bubble gum in.

'Destiny aye? If you have a child, you can call it Beyonce,' I said, smiling sarcastically, before picking up my bags of shopping and leaving. The conversation had been memorable like I'd wanted, but perhaps not for the right reason. Who calls their child Destiny? Dumb shits, that's who.

There was no way I was going to escape what had happened. The house would be a crime scene by morning and I might be arrested by the afternoon, thrown into a jail by the evening and swinging from my shoelaces by midnight. Well, at least I was mentally prepared.

When I got home, I scrubbed myself hard in the shower and put all of my clothes on the hottest wash that my washing machine was capable of. I then called my mother, the only person I knew who would still be awake at this time, because she never really slept.

I listened to her blather on about how she wanted me to move out to Spain and try out her new "shag me silly" cocktail. She also explained, in detail, the problem she was having with her Spanish neighbours. Apparently, they were very inconsiderate and had been swimming in their pool when the house was empty. She only knew this because one of them had apparently left a floater.

The neighbours denied it profusely.

'Well of course they would do. They're foreign; they're not going to own up to leaving a log in my pool,' my mother said, ranting down the phone. I bet her neighbours hadn't actually pooed or even swum in her pool; it was probably their cat who had squatted over the edge and plopped in the pool like I'd seen it do when I was last there.

'How do you even know that there's a floater in your pool in Spain, when you've been at Felicity's house for the past two weeks?'

'Miguel told me, darling. We do more than just sex talk on our daily Skype calls, you know. But how are you dear?' she asked, after an hour of aimlessly talking about herself.

'Tired, I need to go to bed now. Good night.'

After feeding the guinea pigs, I got into bed, but was shaken up by a loud banging on my front door. I ignored it, hoping it was just Oliver. The door banged again, louder this time - so loud in fact, that my neighbours might have heard.

I rushed quietly towards the door, unlocked it and opened it, slowly keeping my hand on the door in case I needed to slam it shut quickly.

'I've come for my guinea pigs,' the man standing at my door said, smiling happily.

'Who are yo- Oh my *god*!' I smacked my mouth. It was Clive! The Mother of Dragons was back from the dead and he was here for my guinea pigs. Well, *his* guinea pigs, but I had adopted them. 'How? I don't-'

'It's ok,' he said softly. 'Your little helium suicide thing didn't work. I woke up a day later with a cracking headache and a sudden burst of life. I want to live - you saved me, Sandra.'

'I don't know what sort of sick game you're playing dude,' I said, pulling him into the flat.

'I'm not playing any game, promise.'

'Then why are you here? Are the pigs here?'

'No. Are *my* pigs here?'

'What?'

'Guinea pigs, you took my guinea pigs.'

'Oh shit, yeah sorry, I did.'

'I'll have them back now.'

'Absolutely, although, I have just bought them a massive bag of food.'

'Perfect! I'll take that too.' He smiled, which would've normally pissed me off, but the evening was so surreal that I wasn't really sure what was going on.

'They're in their cage.'

'Great, do you want some money for the food?'

'No -'

'You must!' He took a £5 note out of his pocket and handed it to me. 'Your assisted suicide attempt has saved my life. I can never repay you enough.'

'You're not going to go to the police?'

'No, there's no need to worry about the police, Sandra.'

As he walked out of my flat with the huge cage of squeaking guinea pigs in his hands, I asked him how he had found my address.

'Before I was, let's say "born again", I spent all my time on the Dark web. I can find anyone with the right tools. Do you need me to find anyone for you?'

'Er, no thanks. By the way, when you say "born again", you don't mean in a religious way, do you?'

'Absolutely! Praise the Lord, I was resurrected like his son and I will live the rest of my life spreading his-' And that's when I slammed the door in his fucking face.

So, not only had I not killed the Mother of Dragons like I'd hoped, I

SANDRA

had turned him to religion - a double fuck up in my book. What had I done differently to Clive that meant that he had survived and Graham and Leanne had died? And what about Doris? Oh fuck.

Had Doris definitely died? She was in for a hell of a shock if she hadn't. God, I hoped to high heaven that that lovely old woman was dead. If she wasn't, she would hopefully grab the gun as soon as she woke up and shoot herself in the face, Romeo and Juliet style. Jesus, what a mess. Maybe it was time to do a runner.

After a lot of deliberation in my third shower of the evening, I decided not to run and instead to act like nothing had happened, in order to arouse zero suspicion. I would just have to internalise my extreme anxiety while keeping a cool and calm composure.

The next day, I left my bag and jacket in the car, went up in the lift and walked into work. I strode straight past the staff room, where I could see Ursula out of the corner of my eye. I had fifteen minutes until I started my shift, but instead of my normal gossip session with Ursula, I went to see Irish Jenny. I rather hoped that her wild, made-up stories would help take my mind off the sight of Frank shooting himself in the face. Ursula would just bang on about her cruise and affair that she was or wasn't having with Alec and I couldn't be bothered with that bollocks this morning.

I cleared my mind as best as I could and smiled as I walked towards Irish Jenny. She had a visitor, who was bending down and getting something out of her bag.

'Hello Jenny, how are you doing today?' I asked. Irish Jenny's recovery was going fine and she was due to be discharged. It was nice to see that she finally had another visitor, that wasn't her poor, verbally abused husband. Hopefully this woman was the mysterious daughter, whose existence Mary and I had a bet on.

'Top of the mornin' to ya, Sandra!' Irish Jenny cheered. I had never heard an Irish person say that before; I'd thought it was just a myth that people from Ireland said that. Similarly, I had never heard Scottish Mary say "och aye the noo". In fact, if I asked her to say it, I'm 100%

sure that she would punch me in my vagina.

Irish Jenny tapped her visitor on the back.

'Selena darling, this is the wonderful receptionist I've been telling you about.' Selena stood up and turned to look at me and introduce herself. She was tall, had long blonde hair and was offensively beautiful.

'This is my daughter,' Jenny said, smiling like a Cheshire cat. Selena (who, by the looks of things had been crying) and I locked eyes. We recognised each other instantly. I dropped my smile.

'Nice to meet you, Se- Selena, if you'll excuse me... I've got to pop back to the reception.' I stumbled over my words and wobbled ever so slightly on my feet as I turned around towards the hallway and made my way down the corridor towards the car park. My hands thumped the wall to keep my balance as I walked as quickly as possible out of the wards and past the staff room. Ursula looked up at me as I stumbled past, but I just smiled and waved.

I rushed to the lift and manically pressed the button.

'Come on, come on!' I turned around to make sure that I wasn't being followed, then the lift doors finally opened. I jumped in and frantically pressed the button for the car park level. The doors closed, and the lift started its ridiculously slow descent.

It was well known that the staff hospital lift was laggy and unpredictable, but today it seemed to be taking the fucking piss. Suddenly, it started to shake, before stopping halfway down the shoot.

'What? No! Come on, come on, come *on*!' I panicked, pushing all the buttons desperately. 'Why hadn't I taken the fucking stairs?' Opening up the phone box that was built into the lift, I saw that the phone cradle was missing the phone receiver. 'Well, of *course* they wouldn't have fucking replaced that! That's just great - don't tell me; the alarm button doesn't work either!' I shouted angrily, slamming the phone box closed and moving my finger down towards the alarm button. If I called the alarm, someone would come and save me, but by that time Selena would have told everyone that I was the strange woman who'd gone into Doris and Frank's house shortly before they'd died. Did anyone know that they were dead yet? Were they both dead yet? I couldn't take the risk.

With an abrupt jolt, the lights and life kicked back into action and the lift continued its journey to the car park.

The lift stopped and the doors opened slowly to reveal Alec, fixing his hair in the door's reflection.

'Sandra! I thought it might've been Ursula... have you seen her? I think she's avoiding me,' he said, as I got out of the lift and he got in. Alec held the doors and looked concernedly at me. 'You alright? You're sweating.'

'It's nothing, just a bug. I've got to go. She's ignoring you because she's married and you're a slime ball. Ok, have a good day,' I said, not turning around to wait for the lift doors close. As I rushed over to my car, I saw the same black Audi from outside my flat parked on the other side of the car park. Had that been there earlier? Why didn't we have designated employee bays, so I could find out whose car it was?

With no time to ponder who the fucking Audi belonged to, I got into my Volvo and made my way out of the car park, faster than a guinea pig escaping from a Korean Restaurant.

29

Roddy

A call came into the station while I was busy reading what The Sun's page 3 model Bethany, 21 from Essex thought about Brexit and Britain's access to the single market.

'Who are you? You're the neighbour, right ok. Well, Ethel, I'm sure that Doris and whatshisname are just sleeping in. Call me if someone dies,' I replied, almost putting the phone down. But then Ethel told me that she thought she'd heard a gunshot the previous evening. At first, she thought it was her husband Reginald farting in his sleep, but his air biscuits were normally followed by a horrendous stench and last night, no smell had ever come. The next morning, Reginald had knocked on Frank's door to ask him if he wanted to play golf, but he hadn't answered. That's when they suspected that something was wrong.

'Right, let's see if anything's happened to old Doris and Frank, via the cafe of course. Dom, bring the Daily Star with you. I need to compare this Bethany bird to the others,' I said, as I walked out the office, jangling my car keys in my hand.

After a lovely big breakfast, we got into Doris and Frank's house (thanks to Dom finding a spare key under the mat). My police senses had already started to tingle. I knew there had been a crime committed and that something wasn't quite right - call it police intuition.

'Doris… Frank...!' I bellowed, walking up the stairs, slowly followed by Reginald, while Dom and Ethel searched the downstairs. 'Everyone, make sure your noses are clear and start smelling for helium!' I instructed everyone before looking at Reginald, who was busy wiping his runny nose with an old hanky.

Everyone started breathing the air in through their noses manically like sniffer dogs during an airport security line up. Meanwhile, I sniffed the wallpaper on the stairs and grimaced at the scent.

'Blimey, it's a bit musty in here. The plot thickens,' I joked to Reginald, who just looked at me, confused. I don't think he heard me properly.

Dom had already finished searching downstairs by the time I'd got halfway up to the next floor. I had delayed as long as possible; after all, I didn't want to be the first one to find something bad. The four of us walked up the stairs with me leading, then snotty Reginald, Dom next, followed by a slow and frightened Ethel up the rear.

'You alright back there, Ethel?' I yelled, but she didn't answer. Maybe she couldn't hear properly either.

I stopped at the top of the stairs, causing everyone else to stop abruptly. They all huffed at me in frustration at my slowness, but I didn't care, I was just scared of what I would find, because I liked old people; they were sweet, like my mother had been before she'd died.

'Can anyone else smell helium? I think I can smell it!'

'Helium doesn't smell of anything, dufus,' Reginald said, pushing me out of the way with one hand while wiping his nose with the other. So, he could hear fine then. 'I'm supposed to be playing golf, not sniffing for an odourless gas in my neighbour's house with you idiots,' he remarked rudely. I thought I'd overlook the one remark and put it down to the stress of the situation, but if he spoke to me like that again, I'd arrest his old snotty arse.

Reginald stepped into the bedroom first and was greeted by a scene similar to one you'd expect to find in a zombie war zone. His body froze for a split second before he warned Ethel that it would be best if she stayed downstairs; something she clearly didn't need to be told twice, because she flew downstairs like a shot.

He should've warned me not to enter either, because when I stepped in and saw Frank's brains all over the wall, I puked up my undigested breakfast all over the floor.

'So much for trying to smell helium,' Reginald remarked, looking at me, disgusted to see my puke spread all over the floor. Dom pushed me out of the doorway, excited about what he was about to see. His eyes fell on the blood and brains, causing his entire body to turn as white as a sheet. Very slowly, he stepped away from the bed.

'Squelch.' His foot squished as he stood on my chewed-up sausage and egg mess on the floor.

Once I had wiped the sick off my mouth with Reginald's snotty hanky that he had kindly given me, I called forensics to get to the scene immediately, as "shit had gone down".

I was right on the case, straight after I had rushed to the toilet to bring up the rest of my Olympic breakfast with apple crumble chaser. Since Dom and I had been investigating Graham and Leanne's suspicious suicides, we had made very little progress; but this new development meant that something a lot bigger was happening. Someone had used a gun instead of just some helium, which made things a lot more dangerous. Hookers could be involve-, maybe even drugs and gangsters, I was excited and afraid, but mainly afraid.

Once Dom and I had contained ourselves and taken statements from Reginald and Ethel, we re-entered the bedroom to see how the forensic team were getting on.

Forensics confirmed that Frank had shot himself rather than having been shot, Doris on the other hand, was a bit trickier. They weren't so sure what the hell happened to her. After half an hour of pondering the situation, I had come up with a solid picture of what had happened. It was obvious that Doris had died in her sleep, kicking the whole thing off, then Frank had found her and shot himself. Case closed. I rubbed my hands together and started thinking about refilling my stomach again. Was 11am too early to be thinking about lunch? I decided that it wasn't.

'So how did the old lady die? Probably the same as Graham and Leanne I suppose...' Dom asked, snapping away on his big camera.

'Listen here, Dumbo. I know you're eager, but don't be, or you'll get yourself into a lot of trouble. It's definitely *not* related to our existing case at all. Now go and get the doughnuts, it's your round,' I said, as I walked down the stairs of Doris and Frank's house. Dom followed me but then stopped midway and looked seriously at me.

'I disagree with you, boss,' he began to say, '...it looks exactly the same as Graham and Leanne. I guarantee she died of the same thing.' How did Dom, the stupid admin bloke, suddenly become the authority figure? I knew deep down that he was probably right, but I had been keen to close both cases quickly. It was getting more complicated every bloody day.

'Of course it is, you plonker. Now let's quickly get doughnuts while forensics do their bit and then we can take over the crime scene,' I laughed through a fake smile.

It wasn't until we were back in the Beemer eating our breakfast doughnuts, when we got the call over the radio from the chief.

'Rodders! There's a woman at the hospital saying she recognised the receptionist woman as the lady who went to the house before Doris and Frank died.'

'God no, please don't be Mary, please don't be Mary.'

'I think it was Mary,' he said, 'Oh no wait, it's the other one. Sandra, is it?'

'Sandra?'

'Get a lid on this one, Rodders.'

'Will do, Chief. But hang on, how does this woman know that Doris and Frank are dead?'

'How the bloody hell should I know?' he said, before hanging up.

30

Sandra

'Oh fuck!' I yelled, realising that I had to be at the airport in 20 minutes and I hadn't even packed or picked Mary up yet. I slammed shut my laptop and ran around my apartment, manically shoving stuff into my suitcase while speed dialling a taxi to the airport.

'You're late,' Mary said, as she got into the back of the taxi next to me.

'Yes, well spotted,' I replied.

'What?' she snapped, as she clicked her seat belt into place.

'Sorry I'm late, for some reason I thought it was tomorrow we were flying.'

'Why would you think it was tomorrow?'

'I don't know, I went into work this morning and then realised-'

'You went into work, on your day off?' Mary gasped, looking very disappointed in me. 'Are you high or something? You only just about go into work when you're meant to, hen.'

I shrugged my shoulders and smiled at her; I was tense, I was always tense when I knew that I was seeing my mother and sister. If you add on to that the guilt of killing an elderly couple in their bed the previous evening, then you could say that I was really fucking tense.

'So, what's the big plan for our fun girls holiday then? Tequila slammers on the plane, strippers in the villa and then a big night on the town?' Mary asked in her thick Scottish accent, smiling widely at me. I saw the driver look at me in the rear-view mirror and smile, but he quickly looked away when we made eye contact. That's right dickhead, eyes on the road.

'Well Mary, first of all I suspect we'll have a sit-down meal with Mother's ex-pat friends, where we'll all discuss the state of a country that none of them live in anymore. Then tomorrow we'll catch a boat out to the middle of the sea and spread my father's ashes, by which time we'll be due for a big family argument, one of us will be thrown overboard and then on the last day you can have tequila slammers.'

Mary sat with a furrowed brow, thinking hard about the itinerary that I had just laid out for us. It must have sounded shit to her, because it sounded fucking horrendous to me.

'Cracking, sounds great. I'll start drinking now!' she said excitedly, taking a hip flask out of her pocket.

31

Roddy

It was only now that someone had made Sandra the main suspect in my suicide-murder case that I finally realised that those helium canisters in the bin might not have been for her balloon business. In fact, thinking about it now, she had been a bit crap at my niece's birthday party, *and* she had been the one that I'd been chatting to on the suicide forum. It was all making sense now. Why hadn't I suspected her before?

According to the woman at the hospital, Sandra had been seen making a speedy dash for the exit and driving away quickly, in what was described as "a right old banger".

'So, we're going to her apartment because we think she might be hiding there?' Dom asked, confused.

'No, we're just popping round for a cup of tea, you bloody idiot.'

'Sorry, boss.'

'Too bloody right. Even if she's not there, we may just find some evidence or clue that will tell us where she is,' I replied, still annoyed at the stupidity of my colleague.

I had considered telling him to get the fuck out for being so stupid, but I decided that I'd deal with him later as I needed another set of hands to help arrest Sandra; she looked quite strong for a woman, and although I could take her down on my own with one quick punch, I wanted someone there - just in case.

RODDY

The second-best thing about being in the police, after the utmost respect everyone had to show you, and the credibility, was that I got to speed around the roads of Malford in my souped-up BMW with the blue lights flashing. If only Mary could see me now, she'd be creaming in her knickers.

Chief had given me Sandra's address via text and Dom had put it in the sat nav as I manically swerved in and out of the cars, even though there were hardly any on the road, and those that were had already gotten out of my way.

'15 Highfield Court,' Dom informed me seriously, trying his best not to do or say anything to piss me off any further.

We abandoned the car on the pavement just outside of the flats and went rushing into the block. I pressed the lift button and waited patiently for it to arrive. Dom entered the block and I watched as he considered taking the stairs because he had a fear of lifts, but he obviously wanted to get into my good books because he waited quietly next to me.

When the lift opened to the third floor, I quickly found number 15 and banged my fist hard against the door.

'Open up, this is the police!' I yelled, secretly loving my new sense of power over Dom.

'Are you sure this is number 15?' Dom asked. 'There's no number on the door.'

'Of course I am you fool, I've been to this flat before.'

'Then why did I have to put the address in the sat nav?'

'What?' I snapped.

'Nothing boss.'

'That's right, nothing boss!' I banged my fist again but there was still no answer. 'Right, this calls for a bit of the Roddy monster,' I said, as I took a few steps back and kicked my foot at the door with all my might.

Unfortunately, my foot got stuck in the cheap wooden door, causing me to lose my balance. Luckily, Dom caught me and helped me pull my foot out of the splintered wood. He then bashed the door in using his shoulder and sent it flying.

Just a few metres away from the door, in the hallway of the flat, stood two young girls under the age of seven. They were both holding each other tightly and both had clearly pissed themselves. Very embarrassing.

'Does Sandra live here?' I barked at the scared girls. They shook their heads and pointed next door. 'Where are your parents?' I asked.

'They took Fluffy out for a walk,' one of them managed to mumble through floods of tears.

'Are you allowed dogs in flats? Why haven't they taken you with them? Anyway, good day to you,' I said picking the door up and placing it carefully against the wall.

Dom bashed down Sandra's door after there was no response to my aggressive knocking. We entered the flat and were greeted by a very tidy apartment with red velvet cushions, a huge bookshelf and an overflowing recycling bin.

'Turn this crap upside down!' I said, curling my top lip in disgust at how much nicer her place was than my own.

'How do we know that it's definitely hers?' Dom asked, as I walked over to the bookcase and picked up the small trophy that she'd won from the pub quiz. Nightmares came flooding back of Mary and Sandra cheering and hugging each other after they'd won the pub quiz. I'd never received a hug from Mary; this Sandra was clearly a total bitch.

'It's hers alright, now get searching,' I said, putting the tiny trophy into my back pocket.

I went to town on stripping the bed, pulling out all of Sandra's underwear from her drawer and scattering everything all over the floor. I even found her dildo and sneakily took a picture of it, but then Dom coughed and I deleted it. I then moved on to search through the kitchen cupboards to find out what the quality of her snacks was like. They weren't too bad; Oreos, Jaffa cakes, Brunch bars, two boxes of

Celebrations (probably leftover from Christmas) and a huge tub of Haribo sweets. She might be a psychotic serial killer with a terrible balloon business, but I'd give her ten out of ten for the contents of her cupboards.

After ten minutes of total chaos, the flat was turned upside down and had started to resemble my own flat. Sandra's telephone rang and the two of us stared at each other. Should we answer it or let it go to voicemail? Before we'd decided what to do, the voicemail beeped and the caller started to leave their message.

'Sandi, I know you're there. I called your mobile again but now it's just going straight to voicemail. I want to talk to you desperately, I need to tell you something.' the man cried down the 'phone. He took a deep breath and let out a huge sigh. 'I still love you and I know you won't be able to forgive me for a long time, but this thing with Claire, it's not the same-' I picked up the phone.

'Hello? What are you doing, trying to graft on a woman who's not interested?' I said, winking at Dom. 'You need to grow a bloody pair mate, she's clearly over you!' I continued, trying to impress Dom with my relationship counselling skills. Dom tried to get my attention, but I completely ignored him. I was in my flow. 'No, I'm not her new bloke, I'm Detective Inspector Benjamin Roddy, the top police dog in Malford! And if you see or speak to her then you need to call me immediately. Oh, and also don't approach her, because she's a killer and she's on the loose,' I said, then slammed the phone down and smiled at Dom, who just shook his head slowly and continued to search through the TV cabinet.

'It might be best not to alert people that she's a killer, boss,' Dom said sheepishly.

'My thoughts exactly, well done Dom.'

The phone rang again and Dom ran over to it, but I got there first.

'I think I'll take this one as well. Go and search the bathroom,' I ordered. Dom walked to the bathroom but said that he wasn't really sure what he was supposed to find in there, apart from bathroom stuff.

In fact, he said that he wasn't entirely sure what we were looking for in the flat at all. Sandra obviously wasn't there, unless she was hiding in a secret cupboard, but there definitely wasn't a secret cupboard because I'd already opened them all on my quest to find chocolate and sweets.

'Hello, who's calling?' I asked formally hoping that it wasn't the ex-husband again. 'Ah hello, Sandra's mother- what do you mean who am I? I'm Detective Inspector Benjamin Roddy. I'm the top police dog in Malford!' I barked, feeling slightly offended that no one seemed to immediately know who I was.

'And can I ask what it is you're doing in my daughter's apartment?' she asked, matter-of-factly. I told her that Sandra wasn't a killer on the loose, but she was a serious person of interest in an ongoing case and it was of the utmost importance that she should tell me where she was or could be.

'I've no idea where my daughter is, she's always had a mind of her own I'm afraid. I don't know if you heard but she tried to kill herself ten months ago - luckily she failed.'

'Yes, I was very sorry to hear that,' I said sincerely, as I started to sit down but then shot back up immediately as the pub quiz trophy had poked me in my arse.

After removing the mini trophy, I sat back down and took some Celebration chocolates out of my pocket.

'And you see, it was very tough for Mummy because I live in Spain with my new husband Miguel. Lovely bloke, can't speak a word of English, but that's ok because he's fluent in sex if you get what I mean,' she said seductively. Yes, I did know what she meant.

'Yes, I'm sure that Sandra is a lovely girl, Mrs. McCutcheon.'

'Mrs. Garcia,' she corrected me.

'Oh, my apologies, Mrs. Garcia. Yes, as I was saying I'm sure your daughter is a lovely girl, but she's also a prime suspect in our investigation and she seems to have gone walkies,' I said chucking another couple of chocolates in my mouth.

RODDY

Janice went on to tell me all about her ex-husband's suicide and more details of Sandra's own suicide attempt. I repeated that I was very sorry to hear about that and was sad when I had read about it in the local newspaper, but then the mood changed when Janice started discussing her marriage to Miguel and how they had recently decided to share their bedroom activities with other people.

'I completely agree love, you *are* in your sexual prime and you shouldn't let anyone tell you otherwise. Tell me please, how are you going about finding these other sexual partners?' I asked, realising that she was deliberately keeping me talking, but I wanted some tips to help me with my pursuit of Scottish Mary. 'I've got this lady you see-' I started to tell her.

'Well, I've found sod all in there, except for a large stash of alcohol and tampons,' Dom said, as he walked out of the bathroom, stuffing his hands into his pockets.

'For God's sake, go and find me some bloody evidence Dom!' I said, failing to cover up the mouthpiece on the phone.

'That's disgusting language, Detective Inspe-' Janice said, before I interrupted her by slamming the phone down.

'I think we should go and interrogate the people at the hospital, see if they know anything about where she's gone.' I filled my pockets with Brunch bars, stepped over the broken door on the floor and waited patiently for the lift down. I'd have to call Janice again later to get that advice on Mary.

32

Sandra

We met my mother and sister next to Felicity's car outside the airport terminal, ready to go on bloody "holibobs", as my mother kept stupidly calling it. We greeted each other with rigid hugs and Mother told me that she'd already checked in her suitcase and confirmed that it was ok for her to carry my father in ash form in her handbag.

'Mary, why are you here?' my mother asked with zero tact.

'Moral support, Janice. Poor Sandra here needs a friend,' Mary replied grabbing my shoulder and bringing me in close for an awkward hug.

'She has her mummy and sister here for her,' Mother replied, looking sheepishly at me.

'And that's why she needs a friend, Janice. I've heard all about you two!' Mary laughed loudly as she picked up her case and wandered into the airport terminal. 'I've heard all about you!'

Mother looked at me, puzzled, as if to say, "she's a bit strange", but I didn't give her the satisfaction of agreeing with her.

'Darling, I just had a very bizarre conversation with a police officer who was in your flat.'

'What?'

'Well, that's what I thought darling. He said you weren't a killer on the loose, but you *are* a prime suspect for something?'

'Are you drunk?'

'Probably, darling.'

I tried my best not to show the look of utter fucking terror that I was feeling, so I instead looked over to Felicity, who was calling her husband to remind him to pick the kids up from their violin lessons.

'Is violin a good idea for a 13-year-old boy?' Mum asked. 'Doesn't he get bullied?'

'The church needs more boys in its orchestra and Father Paul decided that Rupert would be great at it. So, yes, it *is* a good idea for him to learn the violin, Mother,' Felicity said, giving Mum a dirty look.

'Right, I'll meet you in the departure lounge.' Felicity slammed the boot and blew air kisses before rushing off to park her huge 4x4, which was complete with a Zumba mat on the passenger seat to let everyone know that although she was a full-time church mum, she was still very limber.

Mum lit up a cigarette once Felicity had driven out of the gate and down towards the long-stay car park.

'Thank God for that, I've been dying for a fag all week,' she said, puffing deeply on a menthol Superking.

'Why can you smoke in front of me but not Felicity?' I asked, picking up my suitcase. There had always been double standards when it came to how our mum treated us both. Felicity could do and say what she wanted, and Mum would respect it as she had given her grandchildren. Disappointment Queen over here however, had given her nothing but a fucking headache, so I would just have to put up with her minty fag breath.

'Go and check in, darling. Mummy's already done hers. Oh, and don't think this main suspect thing is over. Mummy wants to talk about it more,' she said, waving me away into the terminal like a child.

'I don't call you Mummy,' I muttered angrily to myself, as I dragged the suitcase into the terminal like the exasperated teenager I always turned into when I was with my family.

The airport was packed full of holidaymakers pushing trolleys of suitcases, backpacks, and children towards the check-in desks. I hauled my heavy old case towards the desk and placed my flight ticket and passport on the counter. The check-in assistant let out a loud, bored sigh as she scanned my ticket and looked at my passport, before slamming it back down on the counter. For a moment, my heart stopped in fear that the computer was going to start screaming a warning sound and I would be rugby tackled to the floor by security.

'Put your suitcase on the belt,' she said abruptly, ripping off the label to attach to my suitcase.

'Did you pack the bag yourself?'

'Yes,' I replied, trying to calm my breath.

'Are any of these prohibited items in your bag?' she asked, pointing to the sign full of icons in front of her. I looked at the sign and could make out the knives, guns, flammable and toxic symbols, but the rest looked like squiggles from a bunch of primary school children who were designing their future tattoos.

'No,' I said, as my phone began to ring in my pocket. It was my mother. 'Mother, I'm at the check-in desk.'

'Madam, you need to terminate your phone call immediately!' the check-in assistant shouted sternly, raising out of her seat and pointing at the mobile in my hand. I slowly brought my phone down from my face and ended the call, while staring at the assistant, who was frozen to the spot, pointing at the phone.

'Ok, it's in my pocket now.' The assistant sat down and resumed her "couldn't give a shit" demeanour as she stuck the label on the suitcase and sent it wobbling down the conveyor belt.

'Next,' she mumbled, leaning to see past me for the next person in the queue. I made my way towards customs where my mother was waving wildly at me to get my attention. I looked back at the assistant to see if she was talking to security, but she was busy pointing at the banned substances sign in front of her for the two elderly travellers, who were having trouble making out what the little symbols were.

I was feeling tense, grouchy and fucking scared, while my mother was giddy and drunk as we shuffled along the queue at customs. I had no idea where Mary had gone but wherever she was, I was positive that she was having a better time than me.

Mum put her large handbag onto the conveyor belt, but was told very quickly that she had to put it in a tray. That's when I noticed the litre-bottle of orange squash sticking out of her handbag.

'You have to throw that away, Mum,' I sighed, pointing to the bottle as I put my own bag into a tray.

'But I want to drink it!' Mum laughed.

'Well, you'll have to down it then; you can't take it through there.'

'I can't down it, it's orange squash, not whisky. I'll hide it under my jacket,' Mum replied, taking the bottle out of the bag and hiding it under her jacket in the tray. Why did she have a bottle of orange squash? It could be because she might need something to sober her up before getting on the flight, or it could be that it was actually laced with vodka and her special ingredient; more vodka.

'No Mum, after 14 years of strict airport procedures you should know by now that you can't just hide your large bottle of squash.'

'But I know it's alright, there's no bad stuff in it, it's just orange squash Darling,' Mum replied, laughing it off.

A large, short-haired lesbian-looking woman walked over to the tray and pulled the bottle out. She mic-dropped it into the bin while giving Mum a stern, dirty look. Mum gasped in shock and covered her breasts with her hands.

'For all they know it could be a bottle of acid or some vital ingredient which you could use to detonate a bomb,' I whispered to her.

'But it's just Robinsons... and quite a bit of Smirnoff,' Mum replied, as she went through the scanner. It screamed loudly at her, making her jump and shriek - and cover her breasts again.

The same security guard walked over to her, then guided her over to the side. 'Just because I can't take my homemade squash on board doesn't stop the pilot from flying us into the side of a mountain at 400 mph does it?' she laughed, looking at the butch security guard.

'Excuse me madam, what did you just say?' the security guard asked seriously, taking her metal detector out from her large tool belt.

'Oh, nothing.' Mum giggled nervously while looking worriedly at me as I walked through the scanner with no disruptions.

'Take these off,' the guard said, pointing to Mum's neck.

'They're necklaces, not machetes,'

'Mother, just do what she says,' I said as calmly as I could, through gritted teeth. My mother had clearly forgotten about the lack of sense of humour that England's airport security team had.

'Arms out.' Mum put her arms out in front of her. 'Not like that,' the security guard said. Annoyed, she pulled Mum's arms out to the side roughly.

'Less like Thriller, more like Jesus?' Mum laughed, trying to diffuse the situation. The security guard stopped searching Mum with the metal detector and called over another lesbian-looking guard with a buzz cut.

'We're going to have to privately search you, madam.'

'Can I have a woman do it?' Mum asked worriedly, as she was ushered towards the private searching room.

'This way, madam,' the security guard said, ignoring her.

During my bloody mother's inspection, I waited outside the private searching room for a good ten minutes. Eventually, she and the guards walked out of the room, laughing and joking with each other. My mother shrugged her shoulders and smiled as she held out her magnetic knee supports to show me what the problem was, but I was less than fucking impressed.

'I forgot to take my magnetic knee straps off! Silly me.' Mum shoved the knee straps into her handbag and pulled me in closer to her. 'Sweetie, I think those two men were women,' she whispered into my ear. I just looked at her and walked off. Where the fuck was Felicity and why wasn't she here to put up with *our* bloody mother?

The two of us browsed around the only small duty-free shop in the airport, which I hated and Mother loved.

SANDRA

'Sandi! Do we need a large Toblerone?' Mum shouted from the other side of the tiny shop.

'Why would we need a large Toblerone?' I shouted back.

'Why are you shouting at me?' Mum shouted.

'You're the other side of the sho- *You* shouted at *me*!' I put down the book that I was looking at and walked over to where my mother had picked up 5 large Toblerones, one of each flavour.

'I don't know which flavour I like,' she said thoughtfully, looking at them all.

'So you're going to buy five?'

'No, *you're* going to buy *me* five. I've packed my purse in my suitcase to make room for your father in my handbag.' Everyone irritated me to a certain extent, but nobody quite like my own mother did. She took the biscuit and the crown, and let me tell you it's a big fucking crown.

'Jihadists hack Twitter accounts,' I read The Telegraph headline aloud. 'Better than hacking people's head off I guess,' I remarked, while standing in the queue to pay £50 for over 5 kilos of pyramid-shaped chocolate. I swore that the only people who bought The Telegraph were holidaymakers who wanted the free bottle of water. Next to The Telegraph lay the Malford Herald, with a picture of Graham staring up at me with his arm around what I assumed was his ex-wife. Obviously, they hadn't been able to get their hands on a more recent photo. I moved further along the queue and tried to get the image of Graham's dead body out of my mind. It was funny how his face had featured on the front page for weeks, but Leanne's had only made it once or twice. Maybe the paper found out that she was a childless singleton and those sorts of women are better off out of society, or maybe they just didn't fit in with the "loveable resident commits suicide" storyline that the paper had going. I was sure that Doris and Frank would be splashed over the front cover very soon.

Felicity had finally decided to join us at the airport's only bar, after she had parked her super-mum-mobile, sent her husband a list of instructions via text and gone for a quick prayer in the prayer room. There were now 10 minutes until we boarded.

'Why did we get here so bloody early?' I moaned, wiping some Toblerone crumbs away from my mouth. I had been told that the flight was at midday, but it was actually at 12:25. I was always told an earlier time, because my mother hated being late. If she was late, she wouldn't have time to check out the local bars and if she didn't have time to check out the local bars, then she would have to remain sober. The mere thought of that was hell for everyone involved.

'Because our mother wanted to get drunk and I wanted to pray,' Felicity retorted. 'I suppose we didn't have to get here quite *this* early though; there are only four flights a day so it's not as if there's a giant queue for customs.'

'There are more than four flights a day, silly,' Mum said, laughing drunkenly into her dirty Martini that she'd said wasn't even half as dirty as she liked it.

'I wish we were going somewhere else instead of Spain,' I said. I hated going to spend time in Spain, as it was a reminder that Mum was now completely fine and happy, while her ex-husband - my father - was in ash form in a sparkly urn in Mother's handbag. It would seem that Felicity had also had more than enough of family time already, as she wandered back over to the prayer room to get another quick one in. What a great Catholic...

'Thank God she's gone! Now sweetie, I meant to ask you about your divorce,' Mum said normally, without even a hint of drunkenness. 'Oh, don't look at me like that. It takes a lot more than four Martinis, three vodkas and a whisky chaser to get me drunk.'

I told her that the divorce had been finalised weeks ago - I had already told her this; she must've been too pissed to listen. After that, there was nothing else to talk about, which she accepted before telling me that she'd had a text from Oliver that very morning, asking her to put a good word in with me.

Finally, the gate opened and we started to queue up in the line, but there was no sign of Felicity or Mary. The smartly-dressed pilot walked passed and winked at Mum, who said she was 80% sure that the pilot was that bloke she had accidentally (on purpose) bumped into on a drunken night out the week before in Malford town centre.

'I'll see you in España Sandra!' Mary shouted at us from the beginning of the line. We'd bought our tickets separately, so we were sitting apart. Even though I'd offered her my seat next to my mother numerous times, she had declined, numerous times.

'Bing bong! Felicity Daniels to the departure desk please, that's Felicity Daniels to the departure desk please. Bing bong!' Felicity swanned past the two of us in the queue and approached the desk assistant, who told her that the airport Priest had requested her to be upgraded to "better-economy" for being such a good Catholic.

Felicity enjoyed an extra 5cms of legroom, unlimited Capri Suns and a complementary read of the Malford Herald, while Mother and I got broken headphones, sod-all legroom and rude remarks from the air hostess. If only we'd known that a few prayers would mean a free upgrade, we might've gone all out and bought some rosary beads as well - although rosary beads just remind me of anal beads, and I wouldn't want to put *them* around my neck.

'I mean, this is ridiculous! I've slept with the pilot and I'm shoved in cattle class while my youngest child is given the special treatment,' Mother complained, as she tried to put on her seatbelt complete with chewing gum stuck to it. 'Oh, for goodness sake!' she shouted, as she flung her seatbelt away, hitting the person next to her. 'Oh gosh, I'm so sorry!'

'It's fine,' the beefcake sat next to her said, passing it back.

'Oh my, do you work out?' Mum asked, admiring his massive arms and giving them a squeeze. It was true, the man sat next to her was a very beautiful specimen - an Adonis if you will, but Mother touching him like that made me want to puke.

'Yes I do, but I'm gay,' he said, laughing. Mum's bright eyes and smile dropped like an anvil. 'Well Mr Gay UK, if you could give me a bit more room then maybe I could put my belt on!' she snapped, clicking the offending object into place and moving nearer to me, as I laughed to myself in despair.

At 30,000 feet up, I felt like I was free, even though I was next to my smothering mother in a metal tube, with nowhere to escape except the toilet. The sense of freedom felt fantastic all the same. Yes, I had helped Doris kill herself, which caused Frank to shoot himself in front of me, and yes, the police may find out that it was me, but I was on a plane to Spain and I didn't plan on going back to Malford anytime soon. Suddenly, the tiniest, smallest, most minuscule bit of hope fluttered in my stomach. Maybe I was going to get away with this.

33

Roddy

'Would you like to tell me what happened?' I asked Ursula, as I sat sat down at the hospital staff room table and helped myself to one of the dry old pastries that were in the middle. I took one bite, felt the old, dusty, flaky pastry stick to the top of my mouth and immediately put it back where I'd found it.

'I was on my break when I saw Sandra walk past the door just there. Two minutes later she walked back, but this time in a hurry, looking shifty. I opened the door to see what the emergency was, when I saw her pressing the lift button like mad. Once she was inside the lift, I approached the reception temp and asked her what was wrong with Sandra. She told me that she hadn't seen Sandra and that's when I went into the bowel ward and overheard Selena telling her mother, Jenny, about the previous evening.' Ursula addressed me formally, just like the competent police officer I was. She didn't snarl at me like some time-wasting imbecile, like Mary often did.

I sat with a furrowed brow, half listening, while Dom sat next to me taking notes.

'And what happened when you overheard Selena talking to her mum?' I asked, rolling my right hand to get Ursula to hurry up and get to the good bits.

'I apologised and said that I didn't mean to be rude, but could she repeat what she had just said. That's when Selena told me that she'd seen Sandra the previous evening, going into her Godparents' house as she was leaving. Apparently, she'd been acting weird and had a small suitcase with her.'

'And how does she know that her godparents are dead?' I asked. Dom's head shot up from his notepad.

'A blurred picture of their dead bodies in their bed was all over the news. But there's something I didn't tell the police officer on the phone.' She paused as she thought for a moment. 'I also saw Sandra go into the house last night. I was parked down the street and I watched her leave two hours later.'

'Tell me, why were you parked down the street?' I asked her, slightly confused at why she just happened to be outside a crime scene for two hours. Didn't she have a life? Unless, of course, she was in on it as well and it was a huge operation with multiple killers all working in the hospital. The plot thickened.

Apparently, this wasn't the case. She told me that she'd borrowed her husband's Audi to keep an eye on her friend. She'd been following her when she went out just because she was worried that she would try to kill herself again. But then she had noticed that Sandra had been acting peculiarly, so she continued to keep close surveillance on her. That's when she told me about her movements on the nights that Graham and Leanne had died; she'd written them down in a little notebook.

'It didn't make any sense before, but it does now,' she said sadly.

It was Selena's turn. She was warned that we would need to take a formal statement at a later date, but at the moment it was vital that she just told us everything - but skip over the boring bits, we hadn't got all day.

Selena explained what had happened. She'd checked her phone just before she entered the hospital to visit her mother and had seen the blurred picture of her godparents, lying dead in their bed, on Twitter.

'It was horrendous. How could someone *do* that to such a lovely elderly couple?' she said, wiping her puffy red eyes.

I looked over to Dom, who gulped loudly but didn't look up from his notepad. It didn't take me bloody long to suss out who had leaked the picture.

'So, when my mother introduced the receptionist, I recognised her as the same strange woman who had been into Doris and Frank's house just after I left. I don't know whether she's got anything to do with it, but I'd never seen her before and she had a suspicious-looking suitcase. When she rushed out of the ward, I told my mum who she was, and then the midwife said that I should call you guys.'

'Get that midwife back in here again!' I yelled at Dom, who got up and scampered out of the door.

'So, you're saying that Selena didn't want to call the police and that's why Ursula called?' I asked, as soon as Ursula and Dom were back in the staff room. I was trying to make sense of what had happened and work out whether Sandra was the person who had performed these murder-suicides or not. But at the moment there was no clear evidence, apart from Ursula's own personal stalking diary and this crying woman.

It was too much of a coincidence if she wasn't the culprit; she had failed at her own suicide attempt, she was seen at the scene of one of the crimes, she had attended the Crazies-R-Us group and had plenty of empty helium canisters in her bin. I decided that it was definitely her who was behind the assisted suicides, and that I would arrest her and find the hard evidence.

'Yes, the only reason I called was because I was sure that Sandra was-'

Suddenly, my mobile screamed in my pocket.

'Chief, I'm doing very important police work-' I barked down the phone at my boss.

'What is it?' Ursula snapped, looking at me, irritated that she had been interrupted.

'Look, I don't care if there's a cow holding up traffic, I've got a murderer running wild who's more of a risk. Now if you don't mind-'

I bellowed, but then Chief interrupted me with some more news. 'Are you sure?' I stopped talking, my shoulders and jaw dropped, and my eyes widened as I let out a little fart that got stuck between the chair and my bum cheeks. I ended the call and looked down at my phone in disbelief. 'Someone's found Sandra floating under the bridge.'

34

Roddy

Out of Ursula and I, it was difficult to tell who was more shocked at Sandra's body being found in the river underneath the bridge. We'd both rushed out of the staff room, but then I'd reminded Ursula that although I loved spending time with her, she wasn't actually allowed anywhere near the crime scene.

When Dom and I got to the bridge, the place was full of people looking down at the river, watching the forensics team try their best to secure the scene and get the onlookers to bugger off.

'Right everyone, let's go, the show's over,' I said, waving my arms around and pretending that I had the situation under control. 'The situation is under control.'

'No it's not, look, the woman's boot is floating down the river! Don't you need that for evidence?' one onlooker shouted, like we were in some sort of pantomime.

'Oh bollocks... Oy, Dom! Get the boot!' I shouted down at Dom, who ignored me and continued putting police tape around the trees. 'Dom, go and get the bloody boot would you? Come on everyone, like I said, the show's over!' I yelled loudly, holding my arms out and guiding people away from the edge.

'It's not over! It's only just started!' the same onlooker bellowed gleefully. He was clearly thrilled that someone had recently jumped to their death, the sick bastard.

Dom went rushing down the side of the bank next to the bridge to grab the boot, as I made my own slower, clumsier way down the slippery bank. With a muddy arse and skid marks all down my trousers, I approached the forensics team by the edge of the river.

By the time I'd wiped the mud off, Sandra's body had been pulled out of the river and was securely in a small gazebo that the wind was threatening to send up and away into the air.

'Let's see her then,' Dom said, walking into the tiny gazebo that was already full with me, the forensic guy and Sandra's body.

'Get out Dom, there's not enough room for all of us!' I snapped, not moving my eyes away from the wet, dead body.

'I got the boot. Wait, that's-' Dom said, when he eventually got a look at the dead body.

'Yes it is, now get out before we have two dead bodies in here,' I said in an unusually emotional tone. It really was turning out to be quite a day.

Dom stepped outside, still holding onto the boot, and sat down on the bankside.

'She was found by a dog walker,' the forensic guy said, as he started to inspect the body.

'What the hell is this? You said that Sandra had killed herself!' I yelled.

'Yeah, and she did, *durr*,' he replied, pointing to the dead body on the floor. 'She clearly jumped from the bridge and then "Wheeeee!" She smacked the water and now she's dead. What bit of that confuses you?'

'That's not Sandra,' I spat at him. 'That's Mitzi.'

'Who?'

'Mitzi, the crazy-thin, brown-haired, white woman who is completely loopy. Sandra, on the other hand, is a slightly chubby, brown-haired, white woman, who is only half as loopy as Mitzi.'

'So, I'm supposed to know the weight and loopiness of all the women of Malford, am I? Because that seems to be the only difference here, Rodders. How am I supposed to tell two strangers apart when there's only one physical difference between them?' he laughed.

'Two physical differences actually. One's fatter and has the look of a murderer and the other one is thinner and has the look of someone who has taken lots of drugs.'

'Is this not the killer we're looking for?' Dom asked, poking his head through the tent door.

'Nope. We're looking for a hospital receptionist called Sandra. That woman in there is the kooky nut job from the bloody therapy group,' I replied, annoyed.

'Mitzi,' Dom said.

'Yeah, Mitzi. So, where the hell is Sandra?' I snapped, as a heavy tear finally fell from my eye.

'It's as though she's left the country,' Dom laughed to himself. 'What?' he said, catching me staring at him intently. Well, bugger me, it looked like Dom had finally said something that wasn't completely and utterly stupid.

35

Roddy

After accidently smashing my car door off because Dom hadn't closed it before I'd sped away from the bridge, we finally reached the airport. I abandoned the Beemer right outside the airport and charged up to the terminal. I was Detective Inspector Big Balls, so if I wanted to leave my vehicle outside the airport, then I bloody well would.

As I rushed up the stairs, I might have tripped a little, but only Dom noticed; and he was on his best behaviour, so he didn't even smile.

Bursting through the doors like two badasses in an American cop show, Dom and I charged our way over to the check-in desk and then politely joined the queue. Yes, we wanted to catch a murderer, but the British law of queuing was to be abided by at all times.

'Boss, I don't think we should like be queuing. This is an emergency, isn't it?' Dom said, taking some initiative and pushing his way to the front. 'Excuse me, this is an emergency.' he said to the guy who was currently being served at the desk. He was right, what was I thinking?

The check-in assistant jumped up and pointed to the red line a few inches behind where Dom was standing.

'No standing on this side of the line until it's your turn!' she shrieked at Dom.

'It's alright love, we're the police,' I said, approaching the desk and flashing my warrant card. 'We're looking for a very dangerous woman-

RODDY

'-Who's on a flight to Spain?' the security guard said, finishing off my sentence as he approached the desk from behind the check-in assistant.

The check-in assistant sat back down and continued to serve the man who had been at the desk before Dom and I had interrupted him.

An old man standing in the queue left his place, walked up to me and tapped me on the shoulder.

'Excuse me officer, but as a man of the law you'll be aware of the unspoken custom and etiquette of queuing, so I'd appreciate it if you queued up like I have had to,' the old man said. He clearly didn't care if we were looking for a murderer, terrorist or celebrity; a queue was a queue and everyone should respect that. Fair enough, on any other day I would've respected his wishes and queued up with the rest of them, but today was not a normal day.

'I suggest you rejoin the queue and shut the hell up, before I arrest you for obstructing the course of justice,' I said with my chest puffed out, looking down at the man. He grumbled something under his breath and returned to his place in the queue next to his wife, who was less than pleased with her husband's little show.

Anthony the security guard took us into his little office that was full of TV monitors, confiscated items and crisps. I noticed the crisps first.

'So, gentlemen, I'm guessing it was you two screaming at me down the phone earlier?' Anthony said, taking a seat and propping his feet up on his desk like I did in my own office.

'It certainly was, and we want you to understand the situation of this magnitude... wait, no, that's not right... I meant the *magnitude* of this *situation*,' I corrected myself. 'We're looking for a Sandra McCutcheon in connection with a serious crime that happened last night, and we believe she may have tried to board a flight to Spain.'

'Well yes, you're in luck, she *was* on a flight to Spain.'

'So, I'm guessing you've grounded all planes from Malford and have her held somewhere?' I asked, with my legs spread wide apart and my hands in my pockets.

Anthony started to laugh. A small snigger at first, but then a huge laugh. He brought his legs off the table and held his stomach as he rolled around in a fit of laughter.

'You think that I've grounded all flights after getting a call from two hysterical morons? Oh stop, you're too much!' he said, still laughing. 'Tell me Roddy, what did this lady do?' he asked.

'That's none of your business-' Dom started to say.

'-He wasn't asking you, twonkface!' I snapped at Dom. His recent hobby of brown-nosing me was becoming bloody annoying. 'That's none of your business,' I said, looking sternly at Anthony.

My head started to fill with fire and rage. I'd got so close to catching her and this laughing twat in front of me was taking the bloody piss.

'Listen here, douchebag!' I said, leaning over him and grabbing his collar, before yelling at him just a few centimetres away from his face. 'You'd better get the pilot on the phone and tell him to turn his plane around, because we need that woman arrested before she kills again! So, stop laughing like a faggot and start taking this shit seriously!' I let go of Anthony's collar and shoved him back in his chair.

After a lot of faffing from the security guard, he told us that it wasn't possible, but perhaps the Spanish police could meet her off the plane at the other end?

I speed-dialled the Spanish police quickly on my mobile. Sometimes, when I had a bit of free time, I would add every country's police force number into my contacts. 'Hola, it's Roddy here, I need an armed response unit at Malaga airport pronto. They need to arrest a woman who is currently fleeing from Britain… what do you mean you don't speak English? Is there anyone there who does?' I snapped down the phone, getting more irritated by the minute. My doctor had told me not to raise my blood pressure anymore, otherwise I was at risk of having a really big heart attack.

'Boss, I've got Google translate,' Dom said, getting his mobile out of his pocket and fumbling about with it until the app appeared. 'Just say what you want to say and it will read it out in Spanish,' he said, looking rather pleased with himself.

I didn't like the idea of using a translation app; why couldn't everyone just speak bloody English?

'Right, here we go,' I said, licking my lips and holding the mobile near to my mouth. 'Hola, it's Roddy here, I need an armed response unit at Malaga airport to arrest a woman who is currently fleeing from Britain,' I said, then watched Dom's mobile as it translated it into Spanish. I pressed the play button and Dom's phone burst into life with the translation. I quickly held both mobiles together so that the Spanish police could hear.

'It looks like the phones are kissing,' I joked, but Dom ignored me.

After I'd repeated what I had said in smaller stages and played the translation to the Spanish police, they confirmed that they were now 80% sure what I was saying. I got Dom to send through Sandra's details and I told him to mention that she was a slippery fish, so it might be best to get an armed response unit at the scene.

36

Roddy

I was having the worst time. I'd seen an old man's brains splattered all over his wife, Dom had leaked a photo of said splattered brains, we'd missed Sandra getting on the plane and I'd missed lunch, which I'd never done before, *ever*.

Dom and I sat opposite each other, both bent over our knees, in complete silence. Poor me; I'd never felt so stupid and useless as I did right at that moment - and hungry, I was also very hungry. My belly rumbled loudly and Dom looked up to see me looking sad and defeated.

'Do you want my Twix?' he asked, as he pulled his extra-large Twix out of his pocket. He told me that he always kept chocolate in his pocket, because something boring about having diabetes.

'Yes please,' I mumbled as Dom handed it to me. I unwrapped it and ate both bars at once. The chocolaty goodness filled my heart, belly and groin area with a warm, loving feeling.

'I'm never going to get Mary to go out with me,' I said, as I scrunched up the Twix wrapper and put it in my pocket to lick later.

'Boss, you never know, she-' Dom started to say to make me feel better.

'-I've just let her murderous best friend flee the country; she's going to think that I'm a complete twat.'

'Yeah, but...' Dom said, before taking a minute to think of what he

RODDY

could say that would be helpful. 'Maybe she'll find you extremely attractive now that you've found out who the Malford killer is? Yes, she might get away, but the Spanish authorities will catch her at the airport. It's gone international, boss.'

My mobile rang, but it was just the chief telling me about some abandoned car at the airport that could have a bomb in it. I told him I didn't have time for that at the moment, as I was at the airport waiting to hear about a murder suspect in Spain. I told him not to call me again as the line had to be kept clear, but I promised I would look into the suspicious car as soon as Sandra was caught.

'That was the bloody chief telling me something about a car bomb. In Malford? Pff please, nothing happens in Malford,' I said before realising that the fact that we were currently chasing a serial murderer was evidence enough that perhaps things *did* happen in Malford.

Chief told me that an elderly couple had reported the dodgy-looking car outside the airport, after noticing that the passenger door was missing. They didn't know much about car bombs, but they knew that when they'd seen pictures of them on the news, the car always had at least one door blown off.

The flight was close to landing at Malaga airport, so I decided to quickly browse the duty-free shop to take advantage of the large Toblerones.

'Well, I think I'll get five. What are you getting?' I asked, as Dom joined me in the queue.

'I'm getting this new perfume for my wife. She's going to love it,' Dom said smiling.

'You've got a wife?!' I laughed, extremely surprised, as I put my five Toblerones on the counter.

Suddenly my mobile buzzed violently.

'What do you mean she wasn't on the fucking flight?' I shrieked down the phone. The Detective Inspector from Malaga explained that no one called Sandra McCutcheon had got off the plane that had just landed. She had in fact got off the previous flight that had landed over an hour ago.

'Then where the bloody fuck *is* she?' I shrieked, louder and higher than before.

'Maybe there's a friend she knows in Spain?' the Spanish detective asked, before laughing and hanging up the phone.

'Oh, fuck.' The penny dropped, my balls dropped and my Toblerones dropped.

A small tear ran down my face. I was beaten. Dom opened one of my Toblerones, snapped off a triangle and handed it to me. I put it in my mouth and just let it melt on my tongue, while tears ran down my face. I looked at Dom who smiled and rubbed my shoulder kindly. I may have chased a murderer out of the country, but I'd made a friend, even if he was a diabetic idiot who had leaked a picture of a dead elderly couple.

'Why did you leak the photo, Dom?'

'It was an accident, boss.'

'How do you accidentally leak a picture of a dead old couple on Twitter?' I asked, tears still streaming down my face.

'I was sending a backup of the photo from the camera to the cloud and accidentally clicked "share".'

'You were sending a photo to the clouds? What are you talking about Dom?'

'Well-'

'Don't bore me with it now, I'll deal with it later.'

When Dom and I left the airport terminal, we found my Beemer being taken away by a pickup truck on its way to a special compound where it would be destroyed by a controlled explosion. I had completely forgotten that we'd left it outside the building and I'd also completely forgotten about the phone call from Chief, who just happened to be standing right outside, watching my car get taken away, with his hands on his hips and a pipe hanging out of his mouth.

'There you are Rodders, so this car bomb turns out to be *your* police car! A terrible misunderstanding I suspect, but ah well, life isn't all tickety-boo,' he said, as he got into the back of his Bentley and wound down the window.

He apologised to me through his open window. He said I'd told him not to call me, so how was he supposed to get in touch with me about the suspected car bomb? Just because he was the one who had issued me with the car, it didn't mean that he should've recognised it as being the car he'd issued me with.

'Here's £2 each for the bus home. Tutty byes!' he said, chucking the money out of the car window. The coins bounced off my shoes as Chief's Bentley sped towards the hangar, where his private jet was waiting to whisk him off to Santorini.

As Dom picked up the money off the floor, my mobile rung.

'Yes?' I snapped.

'Chief Inspector Blobby?'

'No, it's Chief Inspector Roddy, you bloody imbecile. Who is this?'

'My name is Rafael and I'm calling from the Spanish Police Department.'

37

Sandra

Mother collapsed on the sun lounger with astounding relief. She liked going back to England every couple of months to see perfect Felicity and her perfect grandchildren, but Spain was where the best cocktails, sun, and hot young *amigos* were. Her villa lay in the mountains on the south coast, furnished with a huge amount of land and a generously-sized pool that she went swimming in naked every morning after her breakfast mojitos.

Felicity and I had only agreed to join our mother on her trip back to Spain in order to spread our father's ashes, and while Mary had volunteered to come along for "moral support", I suspected that she just wanted a holiday. We agreed in the car on the way to the villa that at no point were we to discuss my divorce, Mother's colourful sex life or Felicity's churchy bollocks. So, naturally, we had covered all three before the journey was over.

Miguel no longer worked as a waiter as his "sexy English wife" was very rich after inheriting shitloads of money from my dead American father, who had inherited shitloads of money from his dead American parents. Mother and Miguel took long walks along the beach and partied in the town's hottest clubs until the early morning, when they'd both stumble home and carry on the party with their neighbours, also ex-pats.

'We don't know anyone who's still called Pat, do we darling?' Mother asked Miguel, chuckling away at her own joke. No one laughed so she took another gulp of her sparkly cocktail. Since she had been with Miguel, she had started living to the fullest and had rediscovered her youth, her love of nudist swimming and her love of lots and lots of alcoholic beverages.

What with the whole Doris and Frank thing, my mind had been busy going from worrying that the police would find me, to feeling invincible at 30,000 feet and then deciding that I should probably lie low in Spain for a while.

'Let's talk about Sharon's new face, darlings!' Mother shrieked, pouring the three of us bright pink, homosexual cocktails.

'Pass,' Felicity and I said in unison, as Felicity flicked through her travel bible and I lay on the lounger with my eyes shut.

'Lovely,' Mary said happily, as she leaned forward on her deck chair and took all three drinks from Janice's hands.

'Come on Sandi, love, aren't you enjoying it out here? You know you could have this 24/7,' Mother said to me as she danced around on the patio by the pool. There it was, the first of many times that she would mention and hint to me that I should come and live in Spain where she could look after me. No matter how many times I had told her I wasn't going to try to kill myself again, she didn't believe me.

'Once a cheater, always a cheater darling,' she had said, which confused me as it made no sense at all.

'Why don't you want me and the kids to move out here?' Felicity asked, getting fed up of feeling like the second favourite - even though she definitely was the second favourite.

'Because I'm not going to be your full-time babysitter, darling!' Mum snapped. 'Also, it wouldn't be fair to take Rupert out of his violin classes. Don't do that to Mummy's beautiful grandson, darling,' Mother lied, in a puke-worthily cute way as she stuck out her bottom lip like a child.

If I were to live in Spain with Mum it would be doubly fantastic for her, as she was in desperate need of some new friends. Apparently, I would become her BFF - being her daughter was more than enough, thank you. Due to her new sexual prime status, she was constantly on the prowl for fresh meat, which meant that most of the women in her friendship circle had stopped inviting her to things out of fear that she might bed their husbands.

Miguel didn't seem to mind sharing his wife. In fact, he told me that the jealousy excited him and had enriched their sex life even more.

'She so very sexy, your Mumma,' Miguel said to Felicity, as they both watched her dance to Wham beside the pool. I opened one eye and peered over my sunglasses at Miguel, who was sitting on the sun lounger next to me. He was upright, staring at his wife intently with his legs open wide. Both Felicity and I dry heaved and Felicity snapped her travel bible shut. She got up abruptly, telling us that she was off to cleanse her mind in the Spanish churches.

'Jesus fucking Christ, Sandra!' Mary blurted out, upon seeing my mother dancing, 'I don't mean to be funny or anything, but your mum is dead sexy!'

'Mary,' I said calmly, 'would you like me to kill myself again?'

'What do you mean again? You didn't kill yourself properly the first time, that's why you're still here!' She nudged me playfully, bounced her eyebrows up and down and continued to watch my mother dancing, while sipping loudly on her cocktail.

'I meant to say "try to kill myse-"' I turned to Miguel, whose hand was creeping nearer and nearer to his groin.

'Miguel!' I snapped, making him jump and turn to look at me as if he'd been caught doing something he shouldn't.

'What? You cannot say she no sexy Mumma,' he said defensively, gesturing to my mother dancing drunkenly and waving at the three of us, Miguel waved back, giving her what I imagined were his sex eyes. Mary did the same.

'Well, you three make me want to be sick and then swallow it back down again, so I'll be off.' I got up from the lounger and walked into the villa. Miguel got up out of his seat and joined in with dancing to

Wham's "Wake me up before you go go." Mary just sat there watching, bopping her head from side to side.

Although Dad probably seemed like a lifetime ago to Mother, he still had a part in her life; in a picture frame in the downstairs loo. It was especially fitting, seeing as he had always enjoyed spending a large majority of time on the toilet. It was where he would sit and think about life and what had happened in Vietnam - in between bowel movements, of course. Mother had always thought that it wasn't a good thing to constantly be in your own head whilst on the toilet.

'The toilet is for pooping and puking up last night's drunken kebab darling, not pondering life's big questions or dwelling on the past. We need to get you a therapist for that, sweetie.' And get a therapist for him she did.

'It's no good,' my father said after his first appointment. 'He just sits there, staring at me like I'm some animal in a zoo.' He then announced that he was done with therapy; a year later, he was done with life too.

I had a strong suspicion that something bad had happened in Vietnam, besides the general war stuff, as when I had tried to get him to talk about what had happened during the war, he'd never wanted to. Instead, he just kept telling me that "There's no point to life," and "Even good people do bad things." What was most bizarre to me, was that whatever my father did in Vietnam, he had lived with it for decades without trying to kill himself, so it was a big bloody mystery as to why, all of a sudden, he had killed himself over 30 years later.

He had used a thick rope and a garden chair, leaving nothing but his vast amount of money and a note with "I love you" written on it.

'28 years of marriage and two kids who almost gave me a prolapse, and all I get is "I love you." You wait until I get my hands on that prick!' Mum had said after she found the note. She had gone straight to the anger stage of grieving.

The first night of our stay had got off to a bad start when Mother revealed that she had invited a few ex-pats in the area round for a special dinner party. And by a few ex-pats, I mean that she had invited every British couple within a 5-mile radius. There was the couple from Scotland, the couple from Birmingham, Manchester, Cornwall, South London and finally Wales. The men had turned up to enjoy Miguel's wonderful food and beer and the women had turned up to keep an eye on their husbands and see what Janice's children were like.

Felicity told everyone that she'd found some lovely churches on her walk earlier and that one of the priests had asked for help setting up for the daily homeless feeding. She told us that she'd happily agreed to, of course.

'Of course you fucking did,' I mumbled quietly to myself. It wasn't that I was against feeding the homeless, but Felicity always had to look like a fucking angel.

When she had finished, Felicity had then called her husband and children to tell them about her selfless act. Another good deed for the big guy upstairs!

Once everyone was done kissing Felicity's arse, they moved on to the state of immigration, predictably enough.

'It's ridiculous; all the local pubs that used to be near us are closing down because Muslims don't drink alcohol for some stupid reason!' cried the husband of the couple from Birmingham.

'Perhaps it's because people in general aren't going to the pub anymore, they're thinking more about their health and less about getting shitfaced in an establishment that's built on sexism and working men's culture,' I said nonchalantly. 'And another point is that perhaps Muslims don't drink because, for whatever reason, it's against their religion, which whether you agree with it or not, is their prerogative as a human being, so why don't you shut the fuck up and eat your prawn paella?' I added, making everyone fall silent and stare at me. Then, without warning, everyone burst into fits of laughter.

Mum just sat there smiling at me. She was either too drunk to understand what I'd said, or was taking the high ground and ignoring me. The Birmingham husband laughed a lot because he thought that I was joking, so after he'd finished wiping the tears of laughter from his eyes, he continued to blame the Muslims for pushing him out of a country that was quite glad to get rid of him anyway.

'So what part of bonnie Scotland are you from?' Mary asked the Scottish couple who had been sitting next to her, not only because they both came from the same place, but because they were probably the only ones who could 100% understand each other.

'We're from Edinburgh,' the woman of the couple said.

'Edinburgh!' Mary scoffed, nearly choking on her food. 'Just a load of posh twats and hills in Edinburgh. Me, I'm from Govan, Glasgow. Now *that's* proper Scotland, none of this faffy Tory bollocks,' she said, pointing her knife at the couple.

It wasn't long into pudding before the topic of conversation turned to Scottish Independence, and then to the Germans and the war. Everyone besides Miguel, Felicity, Mary and I laughed at the lazy racist jokes that were coming from the Birmingham bloke and my mother's mouths. Miguel didn't understand a word of what they were saying because their regional accents were too strong, plus he was enjoying his prawn paella too much to care.

'More!' he cried, after finishing his plate and helping himself to another large ladle full.

In the morning, I found Mother dancing to Wham medleys yet again while drinking a breakfast cocktail by the pool - her third. Once Mother had finished her morning routine, we all went out to spread Dad's ashes, but not before a trip out to the local town centre that was full of tourists, English breakfasts and Irish bars.

'It's so lovely to be in Spain! So much culture!' Mum shouted, as she got out of the car. Miguel held Mum's handbag (which contained a large urn full of her dead ex-husband's ashes) as she browsed the tourist tat and bought a range of colourful bracelets and hair accessories. Miguel held very tightly onto Dad's ashes in the very sparkly urn, which was the most offensive-colour pink that Mum could probably have found.

Once we'd all had breakfast and said goodbye to Miguel, we made our way to the marina where the luxury yacht was waiting for us. The captain waved happily to us with one hand and balanced a tray with three glasses of champagne on the other.

'Oh, I'm sorry, I thought there were only three of you,' the captain said as the four of us stepped onto the boat.

'Yes, it was meant to be three but this one is here for "moral support" apparently', Mother said, wiggling her fingers like quotation marks.

'Buckle up ladies, it's going to be at least two hours before we get to your chosen destination,' the captain said in his French accent, as Mary quickly grabbed the last glass of bubbly before Felicity could get it.

Great, two hours to get there, one hour pissing about with Dad's ashes, then two hours back. *I think I'll just throw myself overboard now...*

Dad had always said to Mum that when he died, he wanted his ashes spread out to sea near a small island in the middle of the Mediterranean. Why? Well, because apparently it's where he and one of his American friends had ended up stuck when the speedboat that they had commandeered had broken down, leaving them drunk and stranded for three days until someone rescued them.

'Do you think the captain is a bit sexy or a bit saggy?' Mother asked me, once we were all sitting around the table as we slowly made our way out to sea.

'I think *you're* a bit saggy, Mother,' I replied, watching Mary roll a cigarette with her large sausage-like fingers. 'I didn't know you smoked, Mary,' I said.

'I didn't know your mother was such a hot piece of ass,' she replied, winking at Mum, which made Felicity cringe and Mum shift her chair slightly away.

After two hours and four bottles of champagne, we were all rather fed up and drunk, apart from my Mother, who was just getting started.

SANDRA

'Come and dance with Mummy,' she said to the three of us as she strutted her stuff on the deck to the music that was playing inside her head.

Mary started to get up out of her seat, but I grabbed her and sat her back down. I didn't need any more excuses for therapy.

'We're here!' the captain yelled with gusto. We all looked out onto the ocean to see the tiniest bit of land poking its head above the water.

'Is that it?' I said, looking at the land, thinking it wouldn't even fit two, let alone all four of us.

The captain stayed on the yacht as we all tried our best to squeeze on. I've no idea how Dad and his army friend stayed on this tiny thing for three days.

'I'm so happy you're all here. Well, not you, Mary. No offence.'

'None taken, Mrs Garcia.'

'I can't wait for you Sandra to move out here, so we can be a family again,' Mum said, with her eyes shut, clutching her dead husband's urn tightly. 'I remember when I first met your father. His accent and army physique were so erotic that I was horny for him straight away; then I fell pregnant and we got married quickly after, so you wouldn't become a bastard.'

'Not by birth anyway,' Mary muttered, nudging me hard in the side.

'Then I fell pregnant again and everything was perfect. I had two beautiful little daughters, a hot American husband and tits so perky they would've made Kate Moss jealous.'

'Do we really need to hear all of this?' Felicity tutted. This moment was difficult enough for both of us, without being made more so by our mother's little trip down memory lane.

'Yes darling, because the truth is that your Dad and I had amazing sex and it got even better when we introduced his frie-'

'-So how are we going to do this then?' I said, swiftly interrupting my mother's little speech. She said we were each going to take a handful of Dad and throw him in the water. He would then drift off to sea and live happily with the sharks and fishes.

So, we scooped up the ashes from the urn and stood side by side, looking at each other, waiting for someone to go first. Was someone supposed to say something proper? We'd already had the funeral, which had been full of people spewing churchy bollocks, so maybe now it was time to do it our way.

'Mary, sorry, could you put your handful back into the urn? I don't really want you handling my ex-husband,' Mum said to Mary, who was just smiling and rubbing my mother's back tenderly with her empty hand.

'It's ok Janice, this moment is difficult for all of us,' Mary replied, completely ignoring her.

'I miss you Dad,' I said, as I opened my hand and released him softly into the wind. Felicity was next, then Mum.

'Thanks for our 28 years and the incredible shags darling,' she said, as she dramatically opened her hand with gusto, causing the ashes to rush out of her hand, get caught in the wind and fly straight into my face.

'Oh, for fuck's sake, Mother! It's gone in my eyes!' I yelled, trying to wipe the ashes away.

Mary threw her handful out to sea like she was throwing confetti over a newly wedded couple.

'Well, that was lovely,' she said, looking at Mother, who was looking daggers back at her.

We stayed on the tiny bit of land for a few moments longer while I got the ashes out of my eyes, then we made our way back onto the yacht to drink a toast to Dad.

'To James,' Mum said, raising her glass of champagne as we all sat around the table.

'To Dad,' Felicity and I replied. We sipped our bubbles and looked at each other, not saying anything for a moment. Was it warmth and love that we were experiencing towards each other? Or was it hatred and contempt? It was probably the former for a change, but the moment was quickly ruined by the captain and his big announcement.

SANDRA

'I don't want to worry you, but the yacht seems to be broken.'
'What the fuck do you mean it's broken?' I snapped.
'Well, the engine won't start,' he replied.
'That would render a yacht broken,' Mary contributed unhelpfully.
The captain's hands started to shake by his side as a sudden look of dread flooded his face.
'Is it me or is he drunk?' Mother whispered, so that only the three of us could hear.
'Oy mate, are you pissed?' Mary yelled, but the captain ignored her and continued to shake.
'I'd say he was pissed but it's funny if you think about it,' Mary said.
'What part of this is funny, Mary?' I snapped, reaching the end of my short tether.
'Well, the captain's drunk and the yacht has broken down in the same place that your Dad's boat broke down.'
'You're right Mary, that *is* funny.'
'Captain!' Mother yelled unexpectedly. She never shouted because there wasn't normally there anything that could piss her off. However, being stuck on a tiny bit of land with her two daughters and a Scottish lesbian after spreading her dead ex-husband's ashes was obviously just enough to tip her over the edge.
'What is it?' the captain panicked.
'Are you drunk?' she asked sternly. He looked up to the sky and thought for a moment. And then a moment longer. Ten seconds passed and he was still staring at the sky. 'Captain!'
'Yes, hello... Sorry, yes I am drunk,' he replied sheepishly.
'Yes, I thought I'd ordered eight bottles of champagne. We've had about four and there's only two left.'
'How many have you had?' I asked.
'Sorry, I zoned out. Flashbacks to the accident. What did you say?'
'How much have you had to drink?'
'At most two and a bit,' he replied.
'Well that doesn't explain why he's so drunk,' Mother thought aloud.

'Glasses or bottles?' I asked.

'Bottles.'

'Ah,' Mother began, '...no, that still doesn't explain why he's drunk.'

'Listen here dipshit, if you don't get us back to the marina by sundown, I'm going to cut your balls off and wear them as earrings,' Felicity said. She had cracked as well. 'I'm not going to spend another minute near this tiny bit of land with my pissed mother, my suicidal sister and her lesbian colleague, with you drunkenly having flashbacks to an accident.'

'How do you know about the accident? I don't like to talk about it...'

38

Sandra

There must be a God, because the captain managed to get through to someone back at the marina and call for help. That god must be fucking twisted though, because apparently the search and rescue team had another two emergencies to attend to before coming out to get us.

'Let's all drink up then, girls! And Mary,' Mother said, raising her glass. We were all sitting around the table, waiting for the nightmare to be over, while the captain was in the toilet puking up the two-and-a bit-bottles of champagne he had drunk. 'Some people just can't handle their alcohol,' Mother said, without a hint of irony.

'Do we have any cards on board?' Mary asked. 'We could have a wee gamble while we wait to be rescued by what I hope is a boat full of beautiful women, who are at the very least bi-curious.'

'Our family doesn't gamble,' Mother replied, looking at Mary with her classic judgemental stare. 'We do, however, drink.' She poured us all some more champagne, though none of us felt like celebrating.

'What should we talk about?' Mary asked. She clearly wasn't used to uncomfortable silences like our family was.

'Well we could chat about that foul-mouthed outburst from the good little Catholic woman over here,' I suggested, grinning annoyingly at Felicity, who was sat with her arms folded tightly.

'Or we could all talk about our problems like a fun group therapy sesh?' Mum chirped happily. 'I love having a good sesh.'

'Fine, I'll start. I want to get home to my husband, my kids and my priest. I do *not* want to be stuck in the middle of the ocean with you three non-believers,' Felicity said, looking at the three of us confrontationally.

'You want to get back to your priest? What the fuck?' Mary laughed, before taking a large gulp of champagne. 'I want to get back to my fucking TV box sets, not the kiddie-fiddling priest.'

'Sandra, maybe you should talk. You must be used to all this, what with those group therapy sessions Mummy forced you to go to. You *have* been going to them, haven't you darling?'

'I think I need to drink a few more glasses before I feel like sharing with you lot,' I replied, to which Mother immediately got another bottle and topped up my glass. I just wanted to get this shit show out of the fucking way, hire a car, drive north where the tourists never went and find somewhere to rent while I decide what to do next.

'Fine! Mummy will go,' Mum said, which, judging by the sound of the loud sighs, everyone hated. I secretly liked this as a plan though, because if Mum went on as long as she normally did, she would take up all the time talking about completely bollocks - although it would probably more likely be Miguel's bollocks that she talked about. Either way, by the time she'd finished, the rescue boat would be here and we could all go on our merry fucking way.

'Well darlings - and Mary - Miguel's and my incredible sexual romance started when he was working at the local tapas restaurant and wrote his number on the back of the receipt. How your father didn't notice was beyond me, but then again, he failed to notice lots of things about me really.'

'Christ this is boring, can we skip to the sexy parts?' Mary said, downing the rest of her champagne.

'Sorry, yes of course. I've had to have at least twenty sexual health checks since Miguel and I started "banging it out," as you youngsters call it.'

'Holy hell, no Mother!' I yelled, as Felicity got up out of her chair and stormed off to go somewhere else, hopefully overboard.

'Sandra, you can't complain about my colourful sex life,' Mum said seriously.

'Why the fuck not?'

'Don't swear.'

'Sorry.'

'Because, Sandra darling, you put Miguel and me, but mainly me, through so much with your little suicide attempt that we deserve to shag our way around Spain and not feel guilty about it.'

'That's really interesting, Janice. Please, tell me more about how you went about "banging it out",' Mary said, topping up her glass again. I hit her on the arm harder than I had intended. Perhaps when the rescue boat came, I could stay on the little island that Dad had got stuck on and wait there until I was either eaten by sharks or melted away by the burning sun.

Mother continued to tell Mary and I about how hard she'd had it when I'd tried to kill myself. Apparently, when she and Miguel had found out that I was in the hospital after taking the overdose, they'd got on the first flight back to the UK and sat with me every day until I woke up. For the whole week that I was in a coma, Mum apparently didn't touch a drop of alcohol, which was a huge fucking deal. So, naturally, when I woke up she had some serious making up to do.

'But don't worry darling, I quickly went back to the same old drunken, carefree Mummy that you have learnt to tolerate.'

Normally, my mother didn't want to know what was going on in my head. You might think that she would like to know so that she could help sort it out, but she didn't. She didn't want to know what was going on in my head for fear of not being able to help or cope with it. She didn't want it to start affecting the new life she had built for herself.

The only way she felt she could be there for me was if she persuaded me to move out to Spain. Apparently, I wouldn't have to work because everything was super cheap. I could just spend my time having lunches and naked swims. Personally, I'd rather have shot myself in the face, but that wasn't an option my Mother presented.

'It's not that I don't care, because I really do, but sometimes ignorance is bliss, darling,' she had said to me during one of the few conversations we'd had about my failed suicide attempt. Mother's motto in life was, "Ignore all the bad stuff and it will fail to exist, now pass me another flamin' Sambuca."

'Right, well I'm done. Who's next?'

'I'll go!' Mary yelled.

'No!' Mother snapped. 'Come on darling, we're on a boat in the Indian-'

'-Mediterranean,' I corrected her.

'-Ocean. Share what's going on with Mummy and Mary,' Mum chirped, looking slightly concerned at Mary, who had spent the last twenty minutes just smiling at her and shuffling her chair nearer.

'Fine, why the hell not? I've been helping people kill themselves.'

39

Sandra

My mother and Mary remained completely still, staring at me and waiting for the punchline.

'Well, sorry to disappoint, but it's not a joke,' I said, topping up my glass with the remainder of the champagne.

'Sorry darling, I must have misheard you. It sounded awfully like you said you'd been helping people kill themselves,' Mother said, walking over to the ice bowl where the two remaining champagne bottles were.

'That's exactly what she said, Janice. Your daughter is a killer - would you like a hard cuddle to make it go away?'

'Thank you, Mary,' I said, irritated by Mary's lack of tact.

'No worries, hen.'

'Sandra darling, would you mind elaborating for Mummy?'

'Absolutely, Mummy.' I took a long deep breath and exhaled slowly. 'When Dad invited me over for dinner on the night he killed himself, I thought it was odd that he'd invited me around on my own, without Oliver. It was almost as if he'd wanted to talk to me about something private. I naturally thought that it was about your affair.' I pointed at Mother, who just rolled her eyes. She hated me calling it an affair; apparently, it made it sound sordid.

'Obviously, when I got there, I found him hanging in the garage. His face was white and his neck was red raw from the rope. Anyway, on to the good bits. I then realised I was never going to get that image out of my head, nor was I ever going to feel myself again, so I decided to kill myself. Obviously, that went tits up so I was going to be stuck in this unhappy motherfucking world. But then I met Graham.'

'Graham? Darling, you never mentioned him!' Mother said, excited, completely ignoring everything else I had just said.

'No Janice, Graham was the old smelly farmer who killed himself even though he had a loving ex-wife and kids,' Mary said unhelpfully. 'Continue, Sandra.'

'He *didn't* have a loving ex-wife and his kids hadn't seen him for two years. Anyway,' I gave Mary a sharp look, '...he was going to jump off a bridge but I thought it probably wasn't high enough for that and he would just end up paralysing himself, so I offered to help him.'

'Such a caring daughter,' Mum smiled, without a hint of irony.

'I thought I'd use the suicide bag method that you told me about, Mary-'

'-Hang on a fucking minute; you used the method I told you about?'

'Yes.'

'Did you get paid for any of these suicides?'

'No.'

'That's fine then, carry on.'

'Thank you. So, then I agreed to help Graham and he told me that if I fucked it up, he'd come back and haunt me.'

'And has he haunted you, darling?'

'No.'

'So you didn't fuck it up then, Dear?'

'No.'

'After I helped Graham, I helped the Mother of Dragons from Basingstoke and Leanne from my therapy group. And that's when things went wrong.' I paused to take a large sip of my drink and to assess their reactions. Thank God Felicity was still pissing about somewhere else, because she would've been a fucking nightmare to tell this story to.

They sat there with blank expressions, staring at me for a while.

They were clearly shocked, because Mother didn't say anything and it took Mary quite a bit longer than usual to say something rude and inappropriate.

'Let me get this straight here. You're saying you killed that old farmer, that crazy bint Leanne and Khaleesi, the Mother of Dragons, who you say is from Basingstoke?'

'Well, his name was Clive, *is* still Clive actually, because it didn't work and he's still alive.'

'So, you *didn't* kill the Mother of Dragons?'

'No.'

'Right...' Mary replied, looking into her glass of champagne, clearly trying hard to process what I was saying. 'You know, I kind of guessed that you might've had something to do with the suicides.'

'How come?'

'Scottish intuition.'

'Oh, what rubbish!' Mother piped up, having been silent for a while.

'No Janice, I'm being totally serious. I'm not happy that you helped kill those people-

'-Here we go.'

'-But I can see why you did it - that farmer, Leanne and this dragon mother sound like they were absolute fuck bags-'

'Mary!' Mother snapped, which made Mary stop in her tracks and smirk at her.

'Oooooh, sorry Janice!'

'Before we came away, I helped someone else kill themselves, but it went horribly wrong. I mean, she's dead but so is her husband and it was a mess,' I told them, while the graphic scene of Doris and Frank played out in my head.

'Right, well how are you planning on sorting out this mess?' Mother asked me in her stern mothering voice, the one I hated even more than her cutesy mothering voice.

'If we ever get back on land, I'm going to hire a car and drive north.'

'You're going to hire a car?' she replied, with one eyebrow raised cynically as she topped up everyone's drinks.

'Yes.'

'Oh darling, you really don't know what you're doing. You can't hire a car because you need to give your ID over and then the authorities will be able to chase you down, and they'll find you quicker than it takes Miguel to-'

'-Thank you!' I snapped. 'Well, I'll take a train then.'

'No darling, CCTV on trains, you'll take our spare car. Oh sweetie, I'm sorry you had to inherit such an horrendous trait of mine.'

'What?' Mary and I both asked, equally confused.

'The assisted suicides thing,' she said, smiling at us both like we should know exactly what she was talking about. 'Did I not tell you that I helped your father kill himself?'

'What?' I shrieked in disbelief, as my jaw dropped like an anvil.

'Well, fuck me sideways! This is going to be great!' Mary beamed, rubbing her hands together.

40

Sandra

'Mary, stop being so vulgar all the time! It's really not how one should act when stuck in the middle of the ocean after spreading the ashes of a gorgeous woman's dead ex-husband,' Mother said, pouring herself yet more champagne.

'Sorry Janice, I'm just really bloody excited about the story you're about to tell. I mean, it's really rare to be witness to this sort of horrendous family bollocks and not be a part of it yourself-'

'-Enough!' Mother snapped.

'Mum-'

'-Darling, you have to promise that you'll still love Mummy-'

'-Just tell me what happened.'

'Ok darling, *no problemo*, as Miguel would say,' she said, looking unusually fearful. 'On that day your father had invited you round for dinner, I told him that I'd been having an affair with Miguel for the past few months and that's why I'd left.'

The fact that she'd lied to me when she said she hadn't told Dad about her affair wasn't news at all; she had always been a liar.

'Don't mutter under your breath, Sandra. I know I lied to you, but you knew I'd lied to you, so really it wasn't a lie at all.'

'Continue with the story.' I glared at her.

'Your father was actually fairly unmoved by the revelation. In fact, he looked like he'd known about it all along. So, when I asked him what was wrong he handed me a letter that he'd received in the post.' She took a folded piece of paper out of her leather jacket pocket and handed it to me.

Dear James McCutcheon,

It has taken me many years to find you Sir but hopefully I have found the correct man. You were in Vietnam in 1970 with the 25th Infantry diversion? Sorry my English is not good. My mother told me that I have American father with your name, is it you Sir?

You did not marry my mother, and she said she did not look at the night you had together with happy memories. What happened? When she asked about you the big army man said you had run away from Vietnam. What happened?

I live in Hanoi for thirty years and still live here, would you write back at the address at the top?

Thank you , Hathai

'And in English?'

'My dad raped a woman in Vietnam, got her pregnant and then did a runner from the army.'

'Fuck.'

'Yeah...'

'So, your dad was a raping bastard? Fucking hell! I'm starting to regret coming on this little family trip.'

'Yes, thank you Mary,' Mother and I both said at the same time.

Had my dad raped this woman's mother when he was in the US army? Why hadn't he ever mentioned it? Ok, maybe that was a stupid question. What the fuck? No, I don't believe it at all. He wasn't capable of anything like that.

'Darling, are you going to say something?' Mum said after a few seconds.

'What the fuck is she meant to say, Janice? She's just found out her dad's a paedo.'

'I don't know what to say. I can't believe that he'd do anything like that,' I said, re-reading the letter in case I'd missed the part when it was revealed as a big joke.

'I know darling, I couldn't believe it either. He handed me this letter and cried like the little boy I'd married all those years ago.'

'Christ, *both* your parents are paedos, Sandra!' Mary shrieked, completely misunderstanding the entire situation.

'Mary, go and see what Felicity is doing and don't tell her about any of this,' Mum ordered. Mary immediately complied, while trying to hide the smirk on her face.

'So, he gave you this letter, then what?'

'Then he told me he couldn't remember raping a woman in Vietnam and I told him that was absolutely ridiculous - he either did or he didn't - it's not something you'd just forget. But he said that was during his pot phase so maybe he'd blanked out. Anyway darling, long story short, he told me that he couldn't bear the thought of you and Felicity ever finding out, he had nothing to live for, *bla bla bla,* so he asked if I would help him tie the noose around his neck.'

'Just like that?'

'Yes darling. Well, not *just* like that, but I've tried to blank out all of the other bits.' This new horrendous revelation only meant one thing for me: I had turned into my mother.

'Do you think he did it?'

'No. I know he didn't.'

'Then, why did you help him kill himself?'

'Well, I didn't know he was innocent when I did it, did I? So, just before the funeral, I wrote to this Vietnam woman and sent her some money - quite a bit of money actually - and told her that I was so sorry for what my ex-husband had done.'

'That's nice of you, I suppose.'

'That's what I thought darling. Well, at the funeral, I spoke to your father's best man, who was also in the army with him. Before I'd even said anything to him, he told me to watch out for some bad letter in the post because there was a scam going around to all of the soldiers in your father's squadron. Apparently, there's a Vietnamese woman accusing everyone in the squadron of raping her mother in 1971.'

'Holy fuck!'

'I know, darling. I gave that woman 10 million Vietnamese Dong!'

'What?!' I shouted.

'It sounds a lot, but if you bother to work it out, darling, it's only just over £300, so really it's a trip down Waitrose, but that's beside the point.'

'So, dad died for nothing,' I said, looking blankly at the floor and feeling emptier than I had ever felt before.

'Well, not nothing, darling. He was constantly depressed anyway, I had just left him and he said he'd never want anyone else and he'd only stuck around this long for me. So, really, I just hurried up the inevitable.'

'Mother!' Felicity yelled from the other side of the boat. We both looked at each other with dread. I didn't care if she knew about what had happened with Dad, but I didn't want her to find out while I was in the vicinity. I'd never hear the bloody end of it. 'There's a boat!' she yelled, jumping up and down with joy like one of her annoying children.

'I can't fucking see it,' Mary said, looking out at the water on the opposite side of the boat to Felicity.

'Oh gosh, I can see it!' Mum chirped, standing up and pointing to the small speedboat that was coming straight towards us.

'We're not all going to fit on that fucking thing,' Mary said, after turning around and seeing what seemed like a toy-sized speedboat.

On the speedboat were three lifeguards who, even I had to admit, were so fit they looked like they'd come out of one of the dirty magazines Mum used to deliberately leave in the bathroom.

As the boat approached us, Felicity rushed to where we were sitting and grabbed her handbag, ready to get the hell off the boat. Mary just stood there, looking rather disappointed that none of the fit lifeguards were women, and Mother was staring with her jaw on the floor, clearly elated that they were men. Me? I was still ridiculously perplexed with what I'd just been told about my father's suicide.

'*Hola, hermosas mujeres!*' the lifeguards shouted as they pulled up next to us and flung a ladder rope over the side of our boat.

'*Hola hombres sexy!*' Mother shouted back, grabbing the last bottle of champagne out of the fridge. She pushed Felicity out of the way and made her way over to where the rope ladder was.

'Hey! What are you doing?' the captain yelled, appearing from the cabin that he'd been sobering up in for the past couple of hours. 'We can't all fit in a four-man speedboat!' He seemed angry and, by the look of his eyes and hair, really hungover.

'Hola, hablas Español?' one of the Adonises asked the captain.

'No, I'm French.'

'Explains a lot,' Mary quipped.

'Well, Mr. French, we were the first boat ready, so we came here as soon as we could, but don't worry, there is another bigger, better boat coming just behind us, who will rescue the rest of your passengers and your boat.'

'How far behind?' the captain asked.

'About two hours behind, Mr. French.'

'Fantastic, I'll get on first. Boys, catch Mummy now,' Mum said, as she flung herself over the side of the boat, grabbed onto the ladder and climbed down to the safety of the three fit men in the speedboat.

The rope ladder was quickly untied from and hauled back into the boat, giving mother only just enough time to pop open the bottle of champagne before the driver powered it up.

'See you later, darlings! And Mary!' she laughed back, as the boat zoomed away from us with tremendous speed.

Mary, Felicity, the captain and I all looked at each other and then back at mother, who was waving wildly at us as she flung herself onto one of the hot bloke's laps.

Five hours later, the four of us and the broken boat were back in the dock, ready to get off the rescue boat and get some desperately needed food and water. Felicity rushed off immediately and the captain was busy arguing with the rescue crew while Mary and I got our stuff together.

'So Sandra, what are you going to do now?'

'I told you Mary, I'm going to stay in Spain for a bit while I decide what to do in the long run.'

'What? You not coming back to Malford? But what will happen at work? There's no way I'm doing overtime, they can get to fuck. And what about my Fridays that I have off to visit my sister?'

'I'm sure the hospital will do everything to accommodate your social needs.'

'Really?'

'No, not really, Mary.'

I crossed the wooden walkway from the rescue boat to the dock, which was now almost completely pitch black. We'd been out on the water for almost eight hours and it was now late evening. The walkway wasn't as secure as I'd hoped, so when Mary got on it as I reached the end, it wobbled slightly, causing me to lose my balance. My hand immediately reached out in front of me, but was caught by someone on land.

'Thank you,' I said, steadying myself. 'God, that would've really topped off this terrible day.' I looked up to see whose hand I'd grabbed. It was my mother's.

41

Roddy

It had been 48 hours since Sandra had escaped on a plane, and even though I'd told the Spanish authorities to keep an eye out for her, I had heard nothing. Never mind; I wasn't going to let all this drama get in the way of my favourite pub quiz at The Spread Eagle with my favourite Scottish Mary. Lovely, lovely Scottish Mary.

'Where's Mary?' I asked the barman before ordering my usual drink along with Mary's four pints of Carling.

'Who?'

'Scottish Mary, you know, Scottish, lesbian, beautiful?'

'Oh, the one who wins the quiz every week?' he asked.

'Yes,' I replied, irritated.

'She's away this week, gone to Spain to spread some ashes or something.'

'Oh...'

'Looks like you might finally be in a chance with winning the quiz!' he said, pouring my drinks.

'Wait, did you say Spain?'

'Yes.'

'Who's she with?'

'How the hell am I suppose to know? I'm just the barman.'

'Well you knew that she'd gone to Spain! Looks like you're best bloody friends now!' I yelled, before storming out of the pub and rushing back to the station.

I sat at my desk, searching online for the next flight to Spain. If Mary was with Sandra, then she might be at risk of being the next victim, I let out a small whimper at the thought of it. The Spanish authorities might have told me that they would look out for Sandra, but I wasn't going to leave the fate of my beautiful Mary to those stupid Diegos. No. I was going to save her.

I booked the next flight, which was the next morning at 7:30 am, and printed out my ticket. If the flight left at 7:30am, then I'd have to be at the airport for 5:30 to check my stuff in. But then I'd need to get some breakfast - better make it 4:30am then. It was already 9pm now, so I thought I might as well sleep at my desk for a bit, then go straight to the airport in the morning. Yes, that sounded like a good plan.

Dom had been suspended for the past two days. I had had to tell him to get the hell out of my sight before I prosecuted him for leaking the photo of Doris and Frank.

'But when can I come back to work, Boss?' he had asked like a crying little child who had wet themselves.

'When the drama has died down, or when the chief gets back and tells me to unsuspend you, whichever one is later.' I fell asleep with my head leaning on my crossed arms over my desk, to the sweet memory of suspending Dom.

It wasn't the normal fox that hung around outside the station that woke me up a few hours later. It was a loud bang that sounded like it had come from inside the station. I wiped the drool off my chin and got up from my desk chair to inspect the place. I'm a detective inspector, you see; I inspect things.

'Nope, all clear,' I said, after checking the front desk, the toilets and the staff room, before walking back to my office. But then I walked past the evidence room - Ah! Maybe there was someone in there with a knife, about to stab me for my wallet, or something.

'Who's in there?' I bellowed in a deep voice, banging my fist against the door and grabbing my baton with the other hand. 'Don't worry you two, I've got this,' I said to no one in particular, hoping that whoever was in the evidence room wouldn't try anything if they thought there were three of us out here.

I turned the handle slowly, my hand shaking as I tried to take slow, deep breaths to calm myself. I slowly pushed the door ajar, but there was no noise. Even when the automatic lights flickered on, nothing moved. Maybe they were going to jump out at me and take me from behind. Well, two can play at that game.

'Aha! Got ya!' I yelled loudly, flinging the door wide open and bursting into the room with my baton out in front. 'Ow, bollocks!' I whimpered, dropping my baton to the floor and grabbing my foot as I banged it on the helium canister that was on the floor.

No one was in the evidence room. It had been the canister that had created the loud bang when it fell off the shelf. How it fell off the shelf was a bloody mystery though; must have been some sort of poltergeist or something supernatural like that. Someone trying to give me the spooks.

I looked at the helium canister, which still had the tube and mask attached to it. Dom should've taken that off and bagged it properly, but he obviously hadn't bloody bothered. Or had I not bothered? Did I suspend him before or after taking the evidence from Sandra's flat?

It didn't matter whose fault it was. What mattered was that there was no one in the evidence room waiting to stab me in front of my two non-existent colleagues.

Mmm, let's see if we can have a little sing-song.' I picked up the helium canister and took it to my office, with the tube and mask dragging along on the floor behind me.

'Okie dokie, let's have a bit of the Bee Gees,' I said to myself, setting the canister down on the floor and wiping the dirt that had gathered in the mask. I placed it over my face and started to breathe, I took one deep breath, removed the mask and started singing "Night Fever".

'Night fever, night fev-errrr' - Nope. This wasn't working. My voice had the same dulcet tone it always had, so I put the mask back on and took another couple of deep breaths. 'We know how to boogie–' Dammit, still not working properly. *'What am I doing wrong here?'* After breathing into the mask for a minute or so, I realised that I hadn't actually turned the nozzle on the canister. 'Silly me! Right, let's try this again.' I breathed in the helium for a few minutes as I really wanted to get out at least the whole chorus before having to top up again.

Was this on? I was breathing deeply but it felt like it was just normal oxygen. I turned the nozzle all the way and felt the increased pressure rush inside my mouth. Now we're cooking! Best keep it on for a few minutes longer…

42

Sandra

I sat on my bright orange balcony, inhaling my chocolate muffin and sugary latte as I scrolled through the news on the new iPad I'd bought during my recent big shopping spree.

My escape from the Costa del Get-Me-The-Fuck-Out-Of-Here had been relatively easy really. When Mary and I had got off the boat, my mother had been waiting there with Miguel and her "spare car", which wasn't the old banger I had been expecting, but it wasn't a nice car either. It was a Skoda Roomster, a huge box-shaped car with an engine that sounded like it was going to take off everytime it reached 1,000 revs. It was basically a berkmobile, but it was a car nonetheless, plus it had a huge bag on the passenger seat full of money, clothes and prawn paella. Miguel's idea no doubt.

So, I drove to Madrid, sold the car immediately and found a room to rent in a flat above a bakery with a nice Polish woman who smoked a lot of weed. After counting the money that was in the backpack, I realised that I had a good three years to figure out what I was going to do with my life.

Don't worry; I still had the empty, dull, hopeless outlook I've always had, but deep inside there was also a little nugget of hope. At least I thought it was hope; it could have been trapped wind.

Did I regret killing those people? Nah, not one little bit. I did, however, regret that I'd had to move to Spain, a country that is a) too hot, b) full of Brits and c) home to my bloody mother. Note how I've only called her my "bloody mother" and not my "fucking mother" though. Now that she'd helped me escape I'd started to feel the slightest bit of warmth towards her. It was a condition I was sure I'd get over soon.

I was just finishing my muffin when Veronica, the Polish pothead, came out to join me on the balcony with her Tupperware full of supplies. Sitting down next to me, she cracked open the Tupperware and took out some rizlas, a grinder and a small, see-through bag full of weed.

I scrolled down the Malford Herald news page, expecting to see my face with the words "wanted" above it, but it wasn't my face plastered all over the home page. It was Roddy's.

"Local Detective Found Dead", read the headline. "Detective Inspector Benjamin Roddy was found dead at his desk yesterday morning, connected to a helium canister. It is unknown whether he meant to kill himself or not."

I smiled and shook my head. Silly bastard.

'You want?' Veronica asked me, offering me the spliff she'd just rolled. I took it and thanked her. Perhaps my time in Spain wasn't going to be so bad after all.

About the Author

Jenna Wimshurst is a blogger, vlogger and writer of lesbianism, feminism and comedy. She lives in West Sussex with her fiance Suzanne and her three very fluffy guinea pigs, Rufus, Rusty and Dusty.

This is her first fiction novel.

You can connect with me on:
- https://jennawimshurst.com
- https://twitter.com/Jenna_Wims
- https://www.facebook.com/JennaWimshurst

Subscribe to my newsletter:
- http://eepurl.com/ddPxa1

Also by Jenna Wimsurst

How To Be A Lesbian – A Short Comedy Guide
This short satirical book takes a brief and humourous look at lesbian history and culture, from fashion to queer celebrities and from coming out to how lesbians have sex, this guide will not only educate you on the ways of LGBT women, but it will also have you laughing with every page.

"Such a funny read - literally belly laughed through it. Raw, real and hilarious insight into the world of coming out and living your life as a lady lover"

Printed in Great Britain
by Amazon